KEEP YOUR TWIN UP

WEARS VALLEY WITCHES
BOOK THREE

L.A. BORUFF
LORRAINE COOKE

For Laura, Leigh Ann, & Melissa. When they asked for a blessing, God blessed them twice.

LELA

My food looked amazing. Of course it did, though. Ted had cooked it. His food was always delicious, but the thought of eating it made my stomach turn. I'd eaten with Mae and him two or three times now, and each meal had been exquisite.

"Excuse me," I whispered. Mae looked at me worriedly, but Ted just smiled. Aw, how sweet. He stood when I stepped away from the table. Old-fashioned, but sweet.

In the bathroom, I popped a few chalky, chewable stomach tablets from my purse and adjusted the wild red hue of my newly dyed hair before washing my hands and staring at the full-length mirror behind the bathroom door. I'd lost weight from all the food I hadn't been able to eat. Maybe I should find a doctor before it got any worse.

Ugh. That was something on my to-do list, but I really dreaded it. Finding a good doctor was such a chore. I'd have to remember to ask Bertha who she saw.

Sucking in deep breaths, I got my stomach under control and headed back out to dinner to push the food around on my plate. Mae and Ted both looked a bit worried, but neither said anything. I didn't want to worry them.

The next day was the big move, from the camper to the house, and Ted had invited us over for dinner so we didn't have to cook. Bertha had taken Harriet and her friend to some restaurant in Pigeon Forge that was supposed to be a ton of fun.

"Are you sure about moving in with construction still ongoing?" Ted asked before taking a bite of his risotto. "Seems like it could be stressful."

"There's not much left," Mae said as I nodded and made a hole in the middle of my green beans.

Darn it. I'd been fine when we left home. Hungry, even. I was looking forward to a nice Ted dinner. I loved him with Mae and Mae with him. I'd decided to do everything I could to encourage the union.

"Yeah, it's just a bit of paint and some trim work. We'll probably do it ourselves."

We sat in silence for a moment. Not awkward. Just eating. Well, they ate while I dabbed my mouth with my napkin and took a minuscule sip of my sweet tea.

Now that was something I'd discovered since moving to Appalachia that I never wanted to let go of. Sweet tea in a tall glass of ice.

Yum. Seriously.

"We're open to any volunteers," Mae said brightly with a wink toward Ted. "We'd love to have you over for dinner in the new place if you want. Even if you don't come wielding a paintbrush."

He smiled back. "I hate to paint, but somehow I think the time would fly by with you." Oh, gross. That was enough to make me even more nauseated. He really was perfect for Mae. I was only a teensy bit jealous. Mostly I was just happy for her.

"You might even see the ghost." Mae shot me a look that said she wanted me to keep my mouth shut, but I just couldn't.

"Mae. It's been two weeks since you claim to have seen this specter, and nobody else has seen anything. When are you going to admit it was a vivid dream?"

If she was going to be with Ted, he had to get used to being around us. I wasn't going to sugarcoat things just because we were with Mae's new boy toy. That wasn't fair to him.

We were who we were.

Mae's face hardened as she glared at me. "Listen here—"

She was cut off by the doorbell ringing, then a man's voice. "Hello? Ted?"

Ted looked toward the dining room door. "That's my brother." He jumped up and hurried out of the room while Mae and I followed slowly, trying not to look too much like we were eavesdropping.

"Oh, look at this place," Ted's brother said as he stepped into the foyer. He took his hat off and then looked around the foyer. "You've been cleaning."

Ted stepped forward and shushed his brother. I bit back a laugh. Apparently, ol' Teddy boy had taken up better housekeeping habits since he'd met Mae. Too cute.

"Joseph, I have company."

Mae stepped forward, so I followed, staying just behind her. She was Ted's squeeze; I was just the baggage along for dinner. This was her moment to meet the fam.

But Joseph's eyes cut to me in the back.

The second his eyes met mine, my nausea disappeared. Oh, it was probably still there, but it disappeared with the sudden feeling of attraction.

Joseph had gray eyes, close-cut brown hair with a dusting of gray on the sides, and when he smiled at me, he had a dimple on each cheek.

The closely trimmed beard, just a step above stubble, now that was stinking hot.

"Hello," he said in a deep, rumbly voice. I blinked, feeling like a deer caught in headlights.

Mae's voice broke the spell as she stepped forward and introduced herself[1] . I followed, albeit a bit slower.

It was like I'd been hit with a lightning bolt or something. Who knew Ted's brother would have such an effect on me?

"Joseph, this is my girlfriend, Mae."

I only faintly registered that he called her his girlfriend. She hadn't told me they'd had that talk. But then I saw her face and her blush. They *hadn't* talked about it. Mae didn't seem to mind.

"It's a pleasure to meet you." He smiled warmly at my sister, but his gaze kept jumping over her shoulder to look at me.

Mae giggled once, then stepped to the side. "Joseph, please meet my twin sister, Lela."

He moved forward with his hand out, but before I could take it, the door opened again. "Dad?" A little girl stepped into the room. "Did you get my lovey?"

"No, not yet," he said with his gaze still glued to me.

"I'll go!" She ran past us back into the house.

"My daughter," Joseph said as he grasped my hand. "Eleanor."

"She's adorable." And she was. I'd only glanced at her, really, but she'd had his gray eyes and dark hair. "And...her mother?"

Oh, geez, Lela, could you be a little bit more obvious? I'm pretty sure you're drooling.

Mae's voice in my head cut through my stupor and I finally let go of Joseph's hand. "Sorry, that's none of my business."

He opened his mouth to say something, but Ted clapped him on the shoulder. "Have you and Eleanor eaten? We have plenty."

Joseph shook his head, finally looking away from me to turn toward his brother. "No, but we don't want to intrude."

"If I know Eleanor, you'll have to force her out of her bedroom," Ted said as he opened his arms to usher us back toward the dining room.

I was the last one out so I had to whirl around. Hurrying back to my seat, I gulped when Joseph sat directly across from me. He glanced down at Ted. "You spoil her. That's why she loves her room over here." He grinned, letting us all know he wasn't really mad about Ted's treatment of Eleanor.

A few minutes later, after idle chit-chat that I couldn't remember, Eleanor walked in. "I'm hungry." She was about six, with a little button nose that I wanted to boop.

"Come on." Ted jumped up and went into the kitchen. Eleanor and Ted murmured in there.

Joseph grinned and dished up a plate of risotto, scallops, and asparagus. "She won't eat this, and Ted knows that. She has a very particular palate that includes chicken nuggets, macaroni and cheese, and plain cheese on a tortilla that she calls Taco Bell."

We both laughed, but Mae said, "That sounds just like Harriet at that age. How old is she?"

"Four. She's very tall for her age."

Geez, she really was. I'd thought she was older. "Harriet outgrew it. She eats anything and everything now," I added. "Harriet is Mae's daughter."

Mae nodded. "But Lela is a very involved aunt."

I smiled at my sister. She'd always let me be as involved as I'd wanted to be, which was very. Especially given I'd never had any children of my own.

Joseph smiled, too. "I'm sure Eleanor will outgrow it eventually, too. I just wish she'd hurry up."

We all laughed again and the conversation turned to something lighter, like what films we'd watched lately.

It was easy, cozy and Eleanor had definite opinions on films, though they tended to veer toward the Disney variety.

She was delightful. As attracted as I was to Joseph, I was nearly as smitten with his daughter. I wanted to pull her into my arms for a big hug.

"Bathroom!" Eleanor yelled suddenly and launched out of the chair. While she was gone, Joseph leaned toward me over the table.

"My wife died in childbirth, four years ago. Severe pre-eclampsia."

My heart broke for him, for the pain in his eyes. "I'm so sorry," I said, wanting to reach out and touch him. In my line of work, I'd seen it before, too many times for this day and age.

"It's okay." He smiled a little, but it was tinged with sadness. "It's sure not like the movies. You don't move on in six months or a year. It's only been recently I've even entertained the thought of—"

"I'm back," Eleanor announced from the door.

Joseph shot her a look. "You weren't gone long enough to wash your hands."

She sighed and whirled around, then reappeared a few seconds later, shaking water off of her hands."

Joseph got up, took her by the shoulders, and led her out of the room. His voice faded as he went, talking about good hand washing.

Ted chuckled. "He does his best, but it hasn't been easy since Rory died. I've stepped in and helped as much as I could."

My mind whirred with possibilities. I imagined how it might be if Joseph and I hit it off. How I could help with Eleanor.

The rest of the dinner passed in a blur. We mostly let Eleanor entertain us. She had a bubbly, outgoing personality.

"We'd better get going," Mae said gently. "Lots to do tomorrow."

I glanced at my phone. "Oh, my gosh it's after ten." How had the time passed so quickly?

Ted walked us to the door, obviously trying to hide a yawn.

"We'd better go, too," Joseph said. "It's way past Eleanor's bedtime."

"Can't I stay here?" she begged. "It's Friday."

Joseph looked at Ted, and Ted chuckled. "You know I don't mind."

Eleanor squealed and hugged her dad as I opened the front door. She was turned so she could just see outside. "Oh, my gosh."

Turning to see what she was talking about, I stepped on the front porch. Mae and I repeated Eleanor's words. "Oh, my gosh."

The yard was full, and I mean *full* of animals. Rabbits, ducks, chickens, dogs, and cats. A bear with her cubs. Deer.

"Uncle Ted," Eleanor yelled. "You didn't tell me you had a zoo!"

He laughed and came to the door, then stopped dead.

I grabbed my power as fast as I could and pushed it at the animals. *"Get out of here! Please, go."*

I got the fuzzy reply that I'd called them there. *"I'm sorry, I didn't mean to call you. Please go back to your lives."*

They disappeared fairly quickly, but not before I had to reach out and grab Eleanor to keep her from trying to pet a bear cub. She giggled and reached for them. "Please, they look so soft!"

A warm breeze started up. Too warm. Almost like we were standing beside a fire. I sat Eleanor down and looked at Mae in alarm.

Your powers are going crazy, she said. *Control yourself!*

Sucking in a deep breath, I exhaled slowly, pushing away the heat. I looked around to make sure that all the animals were gone before turning back to Mae, Ted, Eleanor, and Joseph. "Well, I'm sure we'll see you soon."

"Yes," Joseph said, his eyes twinkling. "Very soon."

Oh, be still my heart. I had to walk away before my magic listened to my heart and went crazy again.

After slamming the car door behind me, I waited for Mae to say goodbye. When she got in, I looked at her breathlessly. "My magic responds to him."

She sighed and patted my hand. "Or you really liked him and you let your magic go crazy."

After starting the car and backing out of the driveway, she smiled at me. "Sorry, Sis, but don't borrow trouble."

2

MAE

"If you're going to cook steak, at least leave a little blood in it." Bertha spat out her bite into a paper napkin and snarled in disgust.

Clenching my teeth, I bit back the angry retort that had sprung to mind and settled on something a little less confrontational. "I'm sorry that my cooking doesn't meet your standards, Bertha. If you want me to contribute to meals, I guess beggars can't be choosers." Avoiding eye contact with my grumpy aunt, I turned my attention to Lela. "What were you saying?"

"It's nothing important. I was wondering how much those coins we've got stowed away are actually worth." She paused and wiped the corner of her mouth. "Granted, the voices told us not to spend them unless absolutely necessary. But aren't you curious?"

After thinking for a few moments, I grinned. "Of course I'm curious, but I don't want to be tempted by their value." I wasn't sure either of us was strong enough for that temptation.

"Let me get this straight," Harriet piped in. "You all dug up a huge amount of golden coins that are obviously worth a pretty penny, and you didn't even research their value?" She snorted. "If you guys won't do it, I will."

Before we could protest, Harry whipped out her phone and her fingers moved at a dizzying speed. "What did you say they looked like?"

Lela leaned forward and tapped the dining room table with her fingernails. "Well, they were gold. Definitely of Scottish descent. And they had an imprint of a female on one side."

"Wow, I can't believe you remember all of those details," I laughed. "I was distracted by the spooky ghost voices and the chill in the air when we dug them up out of the ground."

"You've seen them since then, though." Lela pretended to punch me in the shoulder. "We moved them to the hole in the wall. Did you not see the details, then?"

"Of course, she didn't notice the details on those old coins." Bertha dropped her fork onto her plate and gave me a wink. "She's too busy daydreaming about her professor friend."

My cheeks reddened, and I tried to hide the smile that spread across my face. "Despite your constant taunting, I'm fully capable of focusing on the world around me and not just Ted. He does have a name, you know. And it's not *professor*."

Sally must've noticed my increased heart rate because she emerged from her small habitat I'd placed on the table. She shimmied up my arm and sat on my shoulder.

"Everything's fine," I whispered. Patting her cool, moist head with my finger, I took another bite of my supposedly over-cooked steak. Hmph. I was a good cook. At least my ex-husband had said so. And if *anyone* was ever going to criticize my meals, it would've been him.

Harriet huffed. "My phone died. We'll have to look up the coins later." She stood and carried her paper plate to the garbage can. Mae and I hadn't decided on a dishwasher, yet so we'd stuck with paper products for quick clean-ups after meals. She wanted the stainless steel dishwasher with the whisper-quiet motor, but I was drawn to the one with a third tray at the top. It'd be the perfect spot to clean Bertha's mason jar lids. We wanted to find one with both, but the only one we'd seen so far had been ridiculously overpriced. It was going to have to wait for a sale.

"Leaving so soon?" Bertha reached out and took Harriet's hand as she walked past the table.

"Don't worry, I'm just going to the trailer to grab a charger and do a little homework. I'll be around all weekend." Harriet kissed Bertha on the top of the head and made her exit.

Lela and I had moved into the house a few days ago. Once the renovations were mostly complete, we were ecstatic to get settled in. Since Bertha had moved back to her house, her temperament had improved, slightly. We all enjoyed the extra space and the privacy of our own bedrooms.

Instead of selling the camper as originally planned, we'd decided to leave it set up for any guests we might have, even though Harriet was the only one who'd used it thus far. She came home from college on the weekends and visited with us. She enjoyed having her own, private space to study, talk on the phone, and watch her favorite TV shows.

Harry's classes weren't too demanding, yet, since the semester had just begun, which allowed her to join us in Wears Valley every single weekend. It wouldn't last as she received more assignments and her on-campus activities picked back up. But for now, I was loving every minute I had to spend with my girl.

Being in Tennessee with Harriet was a dream come true, even though I never imagined I'd live across the country in a mountain town. So far, I had no desire to return to California. Maybe East Tennessee would be our forever home.

Lela's voice snapped me out of my thoughts. "Bertha, I've got a question for you."

Bertha took a swig of her moonshine and petted Lil' Stinky on the head. He always stood at our feet when we ate meals in hopes of catching a stray bite here and there. He was more dog than skunk.

"Alright, shoot." Bertha sat back and eyed Lela.

Lela cleared her throat. "After everything that happened with Jack, something's been bothering me. Why did Susan get away with killing all of those granny witches? The magic punished Jack for just attempting to kill you. How did Susan come out scot-free?"

"Whoa." Bertha stood and carried her paper plate to the garbage can. "That's a pretty in-depth question. How long have you been stewin' on that one?"

Lela turned the kitchen faucet on and grabbed a skillet to clean. "A while. I thought I'd come to some reasonable conclusion on my own, but I've got nothing."

"How is Jack doing, by the way?" Bertha asked, attempting to change the subject.

"Last I heard, she was doing well with her in-patient treatment." I joined them in the kitchen. "According to Constance, she can see a real difference in her overall attitude and mental stability."

"That's good to hear." Bertha grabbed the clean skillet from Lela and dried it with a dish towel.

"Now that you've deflected, are you going to tell us about Susan or not?" Lela never minced words with Bertha.

Our Aunt responded well to Lela's take-no-crap attitude. "Well, to answer your question, all I can say is that it wasn't the same."

Lela turned to Bertha. "What do you mean it wasn't the same. Murder is murder, right?"

"Well, yes and no." Bertha shoved the skillet into a cabinet. "The magic *drove* Susan to…rid the mountains of the evil granny witches. After all, they were trying to kill you and your sister. Y'all were innocent children, and powerful witches to boot."

Bertha crossed her arms and leaned back against the kitchen counter. "Mountain magic can be unpredictable at times. But the one thing you can depend on is its ability to keep everything in balance. The witches she killed were the imbalance."

Lela turned the water off. "There are so many things I still don't understand about granny witches and the mountain magic. It just seems odd to me that there's a mysterious entity that can pick up on motives and intent."

"It sure is mysterious." Bertha played with her long, gray braid. "I don't question it, though. For whatever reason, our family was chosen to carry the granny witch powers. It's our duty to use them wisely and to keep our intentions in check. I've always assumed that the magic is ancestral."

I raised an eyebrow and Bertha could see that I was skeptical.

"When a granny witch passes away, their powers are reabsorbed into the mountains." Bertha shrugged. "It makes sense to me."

Lela tapped her earring as she absorbed the information. "That's logical. Our powers are passed down from our ancestors, so it wouldn't make sense for those powers to just disappear when a granny witch dies."

"So you're saying that the reason Jack was punished by the magic was that she was attempting to kill an innocent person, whereas Susan was eliminating witches who were evil?" I asked. "And the ancestors are likely the ones who made that decision?"

"Yes." Bertha clapped me on the back. "That's exactly right. You're an excellent student, Mae. I'm sure you get that compliment all the time from your professor friend."

Rolling my eyes, I moved Sally back to her moist habitat and walked over to the cast iron cauldron I'd eyed all through dinner. I knew what I'd seen, and I needed the others to know that I wasn't crazy.

Kneeling next to the heavy pot, I rubbed the top with my hands. Nothing happened. Wanting to give it all of my efforts, I rubbed my hands over the inside and outside of the cauldron. Nothing.

"If you think I'm going to stand around and allow you to trick me, you've got another thing coming." Lela huffed and left the room.

She thought I wanted to get her back for the elaborate trick she and Bertha had pulled on me. If I'd wanted to punish them for scaring me, I would've already done it. I wished she'd take it seriously. A ghost had attempted to communicate with us. Well, with me. This was no prank.

I stood and grabbed a bottle of ibuprofen, popping three down my throat. How many had I taken? I'd lost count. That couldn't be good for my stomach, but I had no other choice. The headache wouldn't go away, and I needed to be able to function. Who has time to lay in bed all day with a migraine?

"Are you hurtin', sweetheart?" Bertha walked to my side and rubbed my arm.

"I'll be okay. It's just this stupid headache that won't subside." I rubbed my temples and closed my eyes.

Bertha held the back of her hand against my forehead. "You don't feel feverish. Does anything else hurt?"

I thought for a moment. Nothing else felt bad, just my head. "No. I just keep getting a lot of headaches. There must be something blooming around here. Isn't this the worst place to live for allergies?

"Be that as it may, you shouldn't be getting headaches every day." Bertha crossed her arms and stared at me with concern. "You let me know if they don't get better in a few days. I've got a few home remedies that'll take care of it."

I shuddered at the thought, as Bertha said good night and walked out to her truck. The only remedy Bertha liked to use was moonshine. Well, heck. Maybe the gasoline-like alcohol would burn the pain away.

Surveying the kitchen, I realized that everything was spotless. There was nothing left for me to do. As a former housewife, I always felt the need to keep myself busy. What else could I do with my idle time?

The cauldron caught my eye. One more try wouldn't hurt, would it?

This time, I pulled a throw pillow from the couch and sat on it. Staring at the cauldron, I gently rubbed the outer rim, hoping to summon the ghost I'd seen before. "Come on, I know you're in there."

As I moved my hand from side to side, a flicker of light appeared above the cauldron.

"Yes! I knew you were real. Talk to me." I sat up on my knees and stared at the faint apparition.

Just as the woman's face came into view, she glanced to the side and disappeared out of sight.

"No, don't leave." I rubbed vigorously with both hands, but she was gone.

Seconds later, Harriet burst through the front door. "I forgot to grab my cup."

"Harry, did you see that?" I jumped to my feet and pointed at the cauldron. "Please, tell me you saw her."

Harriet stopped and stared at me as if I had two heads. "Mom, are you okay?"

"Of course I'm okay. I just saw the ghost again." I ran my fingers through my hair and looked back at the cauldron.

"I think it may be time for you to get in bed." Harriet walked to my side and put her arm around my waist. "Those headaches are doing a number on you, aren't they?"

I sighed. "It's not the headaches, Harriet. Why doesn't anyone believe me?"

Harriet led me to my room as if I was a wandering patient in a nursing home.

I was beginning to think that the ghost was messing with me. And I wasn't pleased.

3

LELA

"Everyone, this is Camille Henry. She's a teacher over at the high school." I motioned for Camille to stand. "I investigated some power problems at the last football game a few weeks back, and finally found Camille. She is a newly discovered granny witch who can manipulate electricity." She'd been skeptical. It'd taken some convincing to get her to come at all. That had been weeks ago and she finally came this week.

Everyone oohed and ahhed at Camille's ability. After she'd made her rounds and met everyone, Constance, the leader of Garden Club, stood.

"I need to steer the conversation to something I've been wanting to do." She took a moment for everyone to quieten down and pay attention. When all gazes were glued to Constance, she grinned. "I want to stop being a garden club. It's time to officially revive the Granny Witch Coven." The crowd tittered, most people looking excited. "It's time to start practicing again and revive Wears Valley's reputation as a magical hotspot. According to our legends, we were once the magical cornerstone of, if not the world, a big part of it."

"What about the men?" Ted asked.

"Yeah." George waved his hand. "What about us?"

Constance gave them both a sympathetic look. "Men will be welcome in the coven, but without power, you'll mainly be supporting the witches with power."

That seemed to be accepted, and after more discussion, it was decided that the Granny Witch Coven would be founded in Wears Valley. Everyone had high hopes for this group of witches. Bertha stood and gave the crowd a shrewd glare. "We should focus our energies on helping the community. Our magic should be used for good."

"Agreed," someone shouted. "We will be a force of light."

"How can we help?" I asked. "Besides volunteering our time."

Constance pursed her lips. "Well, thinking about Camille, perhaps there's a way she could power the home of an elderly person who has trouble paying their energy bill. Or fill a generator or something."

Camille nodded eagerly. "I'd love to do that."

"Maybe I could help with providing wood. Do people still have wood stoves for heating their homes?" Mae asked.

The whole room tittered, with a few open laughs. "Sorry," Constance said behind her giggles. "With you not having lived here long, you wouldn't know. Most of the mountain still has fireplaces and wood stoves, so yeah. Definitely wood would help."

"I could help her." Ted beamed over at Mae. "Deliver the wood where it's needed."

How could I help? Healing! "I'd be happy to heal people who can be healed by magic. Anyone who knows about magic. I'm sure I could help them with my power of healing."

The room was filled with agreement and excitement. We had a plan to help the people of Wears Valley, and it felt good. Our first meeting as an official Granny Witch Coven was a success.

After official business, we milled about, eating. Everyone had brought an appetizer, so it felt like a party. It was nice to be part of something bigger than myself and my worries.

"Lela, how are you?" I turned from chatting with Camille to find Leon standing behind me with a big grin on his face.

"Hey, Leon. I'm well. Long time no see." I'd seen him nearly daily while he'd been renovating our new-old home, but he'd been done with the first wave of renovations for a few weeks now.

"I thought you might have more work for me." He shifted from one foot to the other, looking far antsier than I'd ever seen him. Mae and I had grown quite fond of him while he'd been around, but this was unusual.

"You okay, Leon? You seem nervous."

He held up a hand and shook his head. "No, no, I'm fine." He smiled. "It's just that I really enjoyed working with you. For one, your sister's abilities made my job much easier, but it was nice being around you and your family." He looked quickly around. "And the property is magnificent, of course. That old house, the land. It's an old mountain man's dream."

I couldn't help but furrow my brow. "I thought you had like thirty acres higher up on the mountain?"

"I do, I do. Doesn't mean I can't appreciate your place. I've always loved old farmhouses. It was a pleasure to get to work on yours."

That sounded reasonable. Why was I getting serious creeper vibes off of this guy? He'd always seemed so nice before. Sweet, even. I'd even flirted with him for a while. But now, I just felt ill at ease. He'd been shy and cute before.

"Maybe we could have lunch sometime," he said, moving closer to me. My back-of-my-neck alarm bells went off. What was it about him tonight? Maybe he was off his game. Or I was.

"Well, good to see you again," I said, taking a step back. "We want to do the kitchen eventually, and other things in the house. We just want to take a step back and settle in. Make sure we know exactly what and how we want to remodel before we start." I pretended someone over his shoulder was trying to get my attention. "Take care. We'll be in touch."

He nodded and smiled, but it had a forced quality. He extended his hand for me to shake, but I just waved goodbye and walked away, quickening my step as I did.

I looked back one last time to make sure he wasn't following me, then detoured by the food table. I hadn't been able to eat anything thus far, but the encounter with the strange Leon left me a little hungry. I filled up a plate with delicious-looking appetizers, then turned to see Constance watching me with a smirk.

"What?" I asked, taking a bite of the cheesy puff pastry.

"Nothing," she said, eyes twinkling. "Just something about the way you handled yourself with Leon. He seemed a bit taken aback."

I shook my head. "I don't know what it was about him tonight, but something felt off. Like he was coming on too strong. I just wanted to make sure he knew I wasn't interested."

Constance laughed and nodded. "You handled it perfectly. Now let's get to work helping with the healing."

We smiled at each other and clinked glasses, ready for the next task. This was what being part of the Granny Witch Coven felt like: a family, ready to help and protect each other no matter what. I took a deep breath and smiled, knowing everything was going to be alright.

It felt good to have this support system around me. I had a feeling Leon wouldn't be bothering me anytime soon.

And if he did, well...I'd be ready for him.

I smiled and took another bite of the pastry, suddenly feeling much more confident. I was part of something bigger than myself, and that was an incredible feeling.

At least, it felt incredible until my stomach turned on me again. I set the pastry on the plate and bit my lip, trying to swallow back the bile that suddenly burned my throat.

Constance touched my shoulder. "You okay?"

I shook my head. "No, I've been having this stomach thing." Rustling around in my purse, I found my antacids and popped a couple. "At first I thought it was something I ate, but it's just not going away."

Constance pulled out her phone. "I'm texting you the number for my doctor. He's great, and will likely squeeze you in. Go see him."

My phone dinged in my purse. Her text. "Thank you. I've been wondering who in the world I'd go see. Finding a new doctor is such a chore."

"It is," Constance said with a smile. "But he's the best, and I'm sure he'll take good care of you."

I smiled and hugged her. "Thanks again for everything. I'm so lucky to have you as a friend and part of the Granny Witch Coven."

"Anytime," she said, giving me a squeeze. "You know we'll always have your back."

I turned to find Mae and Ted talking near the door. Bertha walked away from them, so I took her place. Smiling at Ted, I said, "Hey, I was curious. Your brother never comes to these meetings, but he's just as much a part of the Garden Club-slash-Wears Valley Coven as you are. Why doesn't he come?"

Ted ducked his head and grinned at me. "Curious about Joseph, eh?"

The blush that rose on my cheeks gave away my interest. "Maybe. A little."

Mae elbowed him. "Aw, leave her alone."

"Joseph does come sometimes. But he spends all his time with Eleanor, and she's too young for all this. We don't have a lot of family left, so he and I are pretty much all Eleanor has. Joseph knows I'm much more interested in all this stuff than he is, so he usually lets me come."

My heart melted at Joseph's devotion to his little girl. "Maybe he can come to one soon."

"Yeah," Mae cut in. "And Eleanor will be old enough before you know it."

The party lasted a while longer, but Mae and I soon left to take Bertha home. She was happy to go. "Got more candy crush to play on my new phone."

We'd created a monster when we'd finally convinced her to go with a cell. It was a nightmare. She was all over the place with it. The poor woman could barely answer it, much less send a text or play a game.

Once home, Mae went off to do some laundry for Harriet, and I decided it was time to go look at those coins again. I'd been putting it off for too long.

The cauldron and grimoire had originally been in the hiding place. The grimoire now rested proudly on the bookshelf in the living room while the cauldron was shined up and in front of the fireplace. Mae was obsessed with getting the supposed ghost to show up again. My silly, crazy sister. She had to have dreamed the first visit, considering it'd been weeks and nothing else had happened.

We'd tried doing spells and potions in the cauldron and so far all had been incredibly successful. It might not have been good for any ghosting, but it was great for potions.

The hiding place they'd come out of had been perfect to put the coins in. We couldn't spend them, and we needed somewhere to keep them safe. In a hidden alcove in the wall was perfect.

I pushed the ancient stone in and heard a click. A secret door opened, revealing an old wooden box stuffed with coins. I smiled and pulled it out. Once the construction had been nearly done, we'd moved the coins in and secured the door, hiding them away from prying eyes.

They certainly were shiny and looked incredibly old. The lure of the possible value...I searched the internet on my tablet and finally found an article.

"I found it," I whispered. "Mae get in here." I had to repeat myself louder for her to hear me and come in from our new utility room off the back of the house.

"What is it?" she asked while folding a pair of pants.

"I found the coins." Turning my tablet, I showed her the picture from the article. The coin in the photo was far more worn than ours. "Mae, that one coin sold for seventeen *thousand* pounds."

Her jaw dropped and she pulled out her phone. After tapping for a second, she whispered, "That's twenty thousand dollars."

"Holy shmow." I sat back and looked at the box. "And we've got dozens of them."

"Yeah, but we still can't sell them." She shrugged. "Rather be poor than haunted by an angry ancestral ghost."

Well, shoot. She was right.

Back to the poorhouse for us Granny Witches. I put the coins back in their hiding place and shrugged as I looked around.

It wasn't so bad here.

4

MAE

The alarm on my phone went off, but I'd already been awake for at least an hour. I'd gone to bed earlier than normal the night before. Once Harriet had left for campus, I'd allowed myself to rest and had fallen asleep around eight. I'd needed the rest apparently.

Turning the annoying sound off, I decided to pull up the search engine on my phone. I couldn't stop thinking about the gold coins and their massive value. Surely they couldn't be worth as much as Lela had determined.

Typing in the words *golden, Scottish, coin,* and *woman,* I scanned the results, quickly finding the information I needed. The coins were rare and from the sixteenth century, whoa. Although I'd assumed the woman on the front was just a generic figure, it turned out that she was Mary Queen of Scots. The coins had been struck in 1555. Mary was beheaded several years later in 1587. Holy shmow. This was insane.

Rubbing my neck, I imagined what a horrible end that would be. Of course, it probably had been fast and less painful than other forms of torture and execution. The rack came to mind.

The thought of being executed only made my head hurt worse. I'd hoped it would get better after a full night's rest, but the pain had only increased. The light from my phone had made it really pound.

Sally slithered out of her habitat and crawled to my pillow. She stared at me with compassion, if salamanders were capable of showing such deep emotions. Her companionship had been surprisingly comforting to me over the past several weeks. We were connected by magic, and she could sense it when I was off.

I opened my hand and allowed her to climb into the center of my palm. "I'm okay, girl. Just a headache, that's all."

She curled up and closed her eyes and I followed suit, using my other arm to block what little light shone around the perimeter of the window.

"Yoo-hoo." Bertha burst into the room and threw open the shades without any warning and certainly no knocking.

I groaned and pulled the blanket over my and Sally's heads. "No."

"What's the matter with you?" Bertha patted my foot. "You're usually up and at 'em by now."

"It's this headache." I buried my face into the pillow after placing Sally back into her habitat. "My head hurts worse today than it did last night."

"All right. Enough is enough." Bertha pulled the blanket from my head. "Get dressed and meet me in the living room."

Not having the energy to argue with my aunt, I willed my body to stand and threw on a pair of comfortable sweats. I glanced in the mirror and was shocked at the dark circles under my eyes and my pale complexion. Maybe something was wrong with me. Something more than a persistent headache. A worry began to worm through the back of my mind. Could it be something significant?

I shuffled into the living room to find Lela curled up on the couch. "What's wrong with her?"

Bertha grabbed her purse and keys from the kitchen counter. "She's just as sick as you. Except it's her stomach, not her head."

What was happening to us? Had Lela and I caught some type of weird mountain disease?

"Come on. Let's go." Bertha bustled us out the door and into her old truck. I tried to protest that I hadn't even brushed my hair, but she wouldn't hear of it.

The drive to the clinic was miserable. Lela grasped her stomach and moaned in pain, while I held my head and tried to block out the sunlight. Each little bump in the road was excruciating, and these old mountain roads were full of bumps, holes, and oh, so many curves. Whose idea had it been to add so many hills to a mountain?

Once Bertha parked at the walk-in clinic, she helped us out of the truck and led us into the waiting area. She filled out the paperwork while Lela and I took a seat and tried to steady our breathing. "Don't puke all over the room," I whispered to my sister. "Not in public."

Not again.

"That was one time and we were seven," she hissed. "Give me a little credit."

I scanned the room and realized that we were the only patients since it was a Monday morning. Most people needing medical care probably had appointments with their regular doctors, unlike us, who didn't have any doctors here. Plus, we preferred to wait until we were knocking on death's door before seeking medical care. Some might call that stubborn, but I called it frugal.

A cracking sound to our left caught my attention, but Lela kept her eyes closed as if she hadn't heard it. I turned just in time to see a water fountain situated between us and the front door burst open. Water shot out from the pipes. It spewed across the waiting room and, just before it hit the ground or us, it froze in midair.

The receptionist at the front desk stood frozen, as still as the water. Her mouth hung open and her face was as white as snow. Poor woman had clearly never seen magic before. I didn't know what to do, besides try to fight off the panic.

Bertha gasped and ran to our sides. She looped her arms through ours and quickly led us back to the truck. Once we were buckled up, Bertha sped out of the parking lot as if we were being chased by Godzilla. The back tires of the truck actually squealed as she flew out onto the main road.

"What was that about?" Lela asked. "Why'd you freeze the water fountain?"

It wasn't like I'd meant to.

"Whatever's going on with you girls, it's not physical. It's magical." Bertha took a sharp turn and headed back up into Wears Valley. "Don't you worry your pretty little heads. I know who can help."

I didn't have the energy or the wherewithal to ask any questions and instead chose to lean my head against the window. Closing my eyes, I prayed that we made it to Bertha's destination before I passed out from the pain. Or made the fluids in her truck freeze. That wouldn't have been good either.

"How far are you taking us?" Lela covered her mouth with her hands, which wasn't a good sign. Maybe she should be sitting by the window.

"Oh, we've still got a ways to go. Just enjoy the scenery," Bertha instructed as she sped higher and higher up the mountain road.

I turned to Lela and noticed that her face was a light shade of green. The curves were getting to her. The higher we went, the tighter they were.

"Bertha, you better pull over." I patted Lela on the leg. "Now."

Bertha did as I asked and I hopped out of the truck, allowing Lela to scoot across and out. She made it just in time and expelled the contents of her stomach under a tree. Cars drove by slowly and passengers strained their necks to see what was going on. Darn rubberneckers. I waved and smiled as if we were a new tourist attraction. Maybe I could charge a fee per car.

Once Lela had puked until she had nothing left inside her body, she shakily crawled back into the truck. This time I made sure she had the window seat. I put my arm around her, and she leaned her head against my shoulder as my head beat a rhythm against my temples.

"Here." Bertha turned the air conditioner up and made sure the center vents pointed in Lela's direction. "You just close your eyes and try to rest, honey."

Lela didn't respond. I hoped that whoever Bertha was taking us to see could help us. We certainly couldn't go on like this much longer. My head was going to crack open, and Lela'd told me she'd lost five pounds. We had a few pounds extra each, but this wasn't the way to lose it.

"I don't remember these roads being this narrow." Bertha squinted and let off the gas.

She was normally a speedster on the mountain roads, familiar with how to drive the hairpin turns, but these were like nothing I'd ever witnessed. The road had gone down to one lane, so she had to be prepared for another car to come around the mountain in the opposite direction at any moment.

Bertha wiped her sweaty palms on her pants, which didn't give me a warm and fuzzy feeling. Glancing over at my ill sister, I hoped that she didn't have to throw up again. If she did, we were all out of luck.

There wasn't room to pull over on the left side of the road, which butted up against the side of the mountain and the right side was a sharp drop-off.

The blaring honk of the truck's horn scared the poop out of me.

"Grab your chicken handles, girls!" Bertha swerved to the right and slammed on her brakes as a compact car came around the curve.

I didn't know what the French horn a *chicken handle* was, so I just grabbed the handle above the window.

Once the car narrowly passed her truck, Bertha left us sitting in the middle of the road as she recovered from the scare. She took a deep breath and rubbed her temples. I'd never seen her so rattled.

"Bertha, you'd better keep us moving." I looked behind us to see if anyone had caught up to us. "This isn't the best place to take a break."

"I know, Mae. I just needed a moment to recover before my pounding heart turned into an actual attack." Bertha put the truck back in drive, and we continued up the mountain.

After what seemed like hours, Bertha finally pulled into a long driveway with thick woods on either side. The driveway took us another couple of miles and turned into a very narrow trail. Just when I thought we couldn't drive any further without plowing down some trees, we came to a stop in front of a small cabin straight out of an episode of Little House on the Prairie.

Bertha got out of the truck and we slid out to follow her up the wooden steps onto the porch. Poor Lela barely had the energy to function so Bertha held her up. My headache was a minuscule bit better since the clinic.

Bertha knocked on the door loudly and we stood, waiting for the mysterious person to invite us in. While we waited, I took in my surroundings. Like Bertha's house, there were several antique pieces on the covered front porch. The rest of the yard, however, was extremely overgrown. Whoever lived here did not care much for landscaping.

The door finally squeaked open and a frail, elderly woman stared up at us. If we'd thought Bertha was old, this woman was ancient. She was bent over, holding herself up with a cane. Her frail frame was covered by a dress that must've been hand-sewn a hundred years ago and there were an endless number of deep wrinkles lining her face.

If Bertha's old, Lela said in my head. *This woman is already dead.*

I fought back a snort, cause she wasn't wrong.

LELA

"WELL, COME IN, THEN." THE WOMAN STEPPED BACK and held the wooden door open, allowing us to enter the cabin. It took every bit of strength I had to put one foot in front of the other. I knew Mae didn't feel much better than I did, but still, I had to lean on her and Bertha, otherwise, I wouldn't make it inside.

The interior of the cabin was much larger than I expected. The walls were lined with bookshelves filled with ancient-looking books and artifacts. There was an old, upright piano in the corner of the room and a large fireplace in the center. How in the world had they gotten a piano all the way up here? That must've been a herculean effort. No way would anybody be getting it out of here. It'd probably be taken back by the mountains when this lady died, along with this cabin and so many others.

I'd been binging a TV show called The Heartland Series while I'd been laid up with my stomach feeling like a roller coaster on top speed. I felt like I knew all about these mountains now.

The woman motioned for us to sit on the couch, which looked surprisingly comfortable. We all shuffled towards the sofa and sunk into its depths. Bertha sat in a chair opposite us, her eyes never leaving the woman's face.

"So," said the woman, "what brings you here today?"

Bertha and Mae exchanged a look before Bertha spoke up. She explained why we'd come. "I think the twins are experiencing some sort of magical sickness. Lela here can't get her stomach to stop rolling and Mae is having a constant, severe headache."

Bertha looked back at us. "Lela, Mae, this is Mrs. Maisie Williams."

"It's nice to meet you, Mrs. Williams," I said, attempting to be polite even though my stomach was killing me. I was on the verge of asking her where her bathroom was when Bertha spoke again.

"Maisie is a seer," she said. "I think she might be able to discern what's wrong with you two."

"Yes, perhaps." She shuffled close and looked deep into my eyes.

"Mrs. Williams? May I use your restroom?"

She tutted. "Call me Maisie. Mrs. Williams was my mother-in-law." She nodded toward a door in the back of the cabin. "Outhouse is out back."

This poor woman still used an outhouse. Oh, no. Surely, we could help her. It was something we could bring to the coven. Between all of us, maybe—

"Get those thoughts out of your head." Maisie had moved over to studying Mae, but she gave me a sharp look, her rheumy eyes tightening. "I don't want anything changed up here. I like my outhouse; I like my fireplace. When I need help, I'll call my sons. They'll take care of me."

"Don't bother," Bertha said from behind Maisie. "She's stubborn."

Maisie snorted and looked back at Bertha. "That's the pot calling the kettle black."

Bertha laughed, a deep throaty chuckle. "I guess it is."

"Anyway," Maisie said, turning back to Mae. "You going to the outhouse?"

I swallowed and assessed my stomach's rolls. "I think I'm okay for the moment."

She nodded curtly and said, "Then let's get to work." She opened her arms, palms up, and made an inviting gesture toward Mae and me. "Hands, please."

Mae and I both placed our hands in Maisie's. She closed her eyes and hummed a low, ancient-sounding tune as she concentrated. After a second, she shuddered then waved in place.

"She's gonna fall," I said with a yelp. Jumping up, I tried to catch her, but my stomach rolled. Bertha got there first as bile rose up the back of my throat. Mae helped Bertha while I stumbled towards the outhouse. I didn't make it in time, but it didn't matter. I'd thrown up so much back on the side of the road that there was hardly anything left in my stomach to come up.

My throat raw and stomach aching, I slowly made my way back inside to find they'd gotten the older woman onto the couch. Maisie opened her eyes and breathed normally again.

"Come sit down," she said, giving me a sympathetic look. "I know what's going on."

"Can we touch you?" Mae asked in a small voice. "We don't want to hurt you."

"Yes, I won't have another vision like that again." She patted the sofa on either side of her. "You need to be helped, and I have your answers."

Mae and I looked at each other before slowly moving toward the couch. We were both scared—scared of what this woman would tell us, what was wrong with us, and how we'd ever get out of this mess.

Maisie smiled, and with it, a calm washed over us both. We sat on either side of her, and she stroked our hands lovingly.

"It'll be okay," she said softly. "Everything will be just fine. You've just gotten too full of magic. I think I can help you get back home, but once you get some-where with some privacy, you need to use a signifi-cant amount of magic."

We gaped at her. "What?" I snapped my mouth shut. "I mean, seriously? We find out we're like these super powerful witches, which is really cool, but now it's making us sick?"

She chuckled. "Nothing comes for free, does it? But this isn't the end of the world, child. You just need to find a way to share your magic. That's all."

"You said you can take some?" Mae asked.

"I'm only a seer. I get visions and feelings. They often overwhelm me, which is why I prefer my mountain cabin to anything down in town."

That made sense, though I didn't see why she couldn't give herself a few more amenities.

"Because the fewer people I have traipsing around up here the better," Maisie answered.

I leaned back and raised my eyebrows. She'd read my mind?

She smiled. "I can't read your thoughts, but I do get an overall sense of what you're feeling and thinking. It's one of the reasons why I'm so attuned to my visions. And why I don't like company."

Mae and I shared a look. We had a lot to learn. Whatever Maisie was going to do to help us, we would do our best to absorb it all. We needed her.

Bertha leaned forward and patted Maisie on the plaid-skirt-covered knee. "Sorry to bust them in on you. I thought their ailments were physical, but then in the clinic, Mae's magic burst out right in front of God and the world."

Maisie chuckled. "That could be a problem. It's fine for you to bring your kin up here, Bertha, you know that. I don't consider fellow granny witches to be company."

"So, what is it you can do to help us?" Mae asked. She patted Maisie on the hand. "Which, by the way, we will appreciate greatly."

"I've already done it." Maisie winked and looked at me. "Is your headache better?" She turned her head to Mae and said, "Your stomach?"

"It's my stomach and her headache, but..." I sucked in a deep breath. "While the nausea and cramps are still there, they're much better."

Maisie nodded. "That's because I absorbed as much as I could. As a seer, I can't take too much, but I've gotten good at siphoning magic off of people. Or at least, I was good at it before you two were born."

"And since we've been back?" I asked. "How have you been?"

Maisie sighed. "It's been wonderful. Like I'd lost an arm and it suddenly grew back."

Bertha nodded. "What an apt way to put it."

Maisie smiled. "Indeed. Now, you two will have to find ways to keep your magic in check and share it with others, however you can. You can come here any time, I'll gladly take whatever I can hold."

My stomach was better, but she hadn't been able to take enough to really give relief. Bless her old heart, she just couldn't hold enough. "We appreciate you so much. Please, if we can ever do anything for you, you only need to ask." I squeezed her hands, very gently because they were turned with arthritis, and stood. "Let's get home before this wears off. I can't face those winding roads with my stomach as sick as it was again." The very thought made me shudder.

Mae gave Maisie a hug, as did Bertha, then we were soon back in the truck. "Let's get home," I said as I kept my eyes on the road. Maybe if I didn't look away, I wouldn't get quite so sick.

It helped a little. By the time we got to the house I was dizzy and nauseated, but didn't feel like I was going to throw up again thank heavens. My stomach muscles couldn't take it.

"What now?" I asked as I lowered myself onto the porch. "How do we share magic?"

I didn't have the first clue how to give someone else some of the magic I only barely knew how to control. But it had to be figured out, and soon.

"What if we just *use* our magic?" Mae asked. "I know I, for one, was using it a ton when Leon was here and the construction was going on."

I nodded. "Yeah, I was outside a lot, and doing a ton with my magic and practicing with the new temperature thing. I haven't been for the last several days, though."

Mae tapped her foot. "Come on." She hauled me to my feet and we traipsed around the house to the backyard. "Call the animals." Throwing up one hand she grinned. "Now, can you call *sick* animals?"

I shrugged. "I can try."

We walked a little deeper into the woods and sat on a grassy hill beside the water. While Mae manipulated the water, moving it in and out and up and down, I called animals to me. Sick, injured, any that would come. When they came close, I healed them of their injuries or illnesses. Most were minor, but a few were difficult enough to really wear me out.

Every animal I healed, my stomach got a little bit better until finally, a couple of hours into the afternoon, I was exhausted and absolutely starving.

Mae beamed at me around a new tree she'd grown between us. "My head feels great. How's your stomach?"

"Hungry."

"Girls," Bertha called from the back porch of the house. "Supper!"

She'd read our minds. We jumped up, and as tired as I felt, I had more energy than I had in days. Maybe weeks. Mae and I clasped hands and rushed toward the house. "Let's eat," I said excitedly. "Now that we know how to control this, we can figure something out."

"Absolutely." Mae swung our hands. "This is going to work out."

6

MAE

"Mae! Coffee's ready," Lela yelled to me from the kitchen while I finished swiping a light pink lipstick on my lips. Taking a hot shower was just what I'd needed. The headache was gone, so I no longer had to avoid the scorching water on my face, which had made the pain worse.

The seer had been right. Offloading our magic provided a release of pent-up magic. I felt lighter this morning, as if I was no longer carrying a heavy burden on my shoulders. Tossing the lipstick into my makeup bag, I headed toward the kitchen. The strong smell of coffee made my stomach growl. I hadn't eaten enough last night to replace the energy lost yesterday. All the plant and water manipulation took a lot of effort. I was ravenous now.

"Good morning, Sunshine." Lela greeted me with a smile.

Good. She was obviously feeling better, as well.

"Good morning, Sis," I greeted her back. "What do you have planned for today?"

Lela sighed. "Honestly, I don't think I have the energy to do much of anything."

She was right. I realized that even though my headache was gone, I felt as if I'd run a marathon. Plopping down onto one of the kitchen counter stools, I poured a cup of coffee and decided to drink it black.

"At least it worked." Lela shrugged and took a sip of her coffee. "It's not sustainable, though."

"What do you mean?" I patted Lil' Stinky, who'd decided to join us in the kitchen. He and Sally had spent yesterday afternoon watching us work our magic, and it had apparently exhausted them just to watch. He hopped onto the counter and stretched like a cat. After a long yawn, he curled up near the warm coffee pot and laid his head on his front paws.

"We must've worn him out, as well." I chuckled as the poor skunk closed his eyes.

Lela nodded. "It took a lot out of us, and I don't think we can do it all the time. We have to find a balance between not letting the magic build up and not exhausting ourselves."

Someone knocked on the front door.

"Come on in, Bertha." I'm not sure why I bothered telling her to enter. She always did, regardless. And who else would be knocking at our door first thing in the morning?

"Mornin' girls." She dropped her purse onto the couch and joined us in the kitchen. "The coffee smells wonderful. I need a pick-me-up after the show you all put on last night."

Lela cleared her throat. "That's what we were discussing, actually. It wore us out."

"I bet it did." Bertha leaned forward onto the counter. "You'd stored up a huge amount of magic. That's not easy to expel in one session."

"What will we do if the magic builds up again?" I asked.

Bertha scratched her head. "I don't know. But you shouldn't offload your magic like that again unless it's absolutely necessary. I'm surprised you two aren't still in bed. Think about the energy you used last night."

"Yeah, that wasn't fun," I agreed. "But what other option do we have? I don't know about Lela, but I can't function with those headaches."

We sipped our coffees in silence for a few moments until our phones buzzed simultaneously.

It was a group text from Constance to our coven.

Coven meeting Friday evening at 7.

"Wait. I think I have an idea." I hopped down from the bar stool and paced the kitchen floor. "Do you think we could share some of our powers with the coven?"

"The coven already has their own powers," Lela pointed out.

"Yes, I know." I crossed my arms. "But what if instead of offloading our powers whenever they build up, we transfer the excess onto some of the coven members before they build up again."

Bertha set her coffee cup on the table. "That just might work since the coven members' powers are much less powerful than yours. They could handle it without getting physical symptoms from too much magic."

"The real question is whether or not it can be done." Lela pushed her red hair behind her ears. "I thought about it yesterday but wouldn't begin to know how to do it."

After thinking for a moment, I walked to the bookshelf and retrieved the grimoire. "Maybe there's a spell that would do the trick."

Bertha stood behind me and peered over my shoulder. "Stop. Look at that one."

The top of the page read *Link Witches Together*.

"That sounds promising." I scanned the page and found that there was a small note in the margin in a different handwriting that said, *also good for sharing power*. "I don't think we'll find a better fit in terms of spells."

"It looks like you've found the answer." Bertha beamed.

"Sounds like we have a plan for Friday night," Lela said with a smile.

We shared a knowing glance and went back to drinking our coffee. We'd figure out how to distribute our magic safely—and hopefully, more sustainably—at the coven meeting.

Fragments of excited energy flowed through me as we finished up our coffee that morning. This was the right solution to our problem, and it felt good to have a plan in motion. We'd be able to use the power within us without worrying about running out of steam or having too much magic building up.

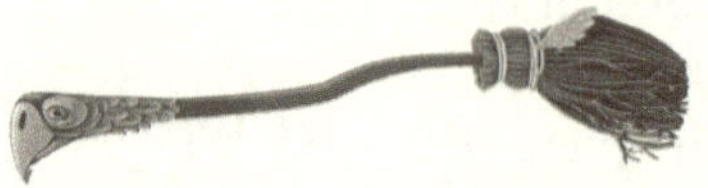

AFTER A TWO-HOUR AFTERNOON NAP, I hoped I had enough energy to converse with Ted on our dinner date. As soon as I saw his smiling face, a bolt of energy ran from my head to my toes. He was so handsome and his personality made him even more attractive. It was all too easy to feel energized.

He'd insisted that we try out an Italian place a few cities over. I still wasn't very familiar with the areas surrounding Wears Valley and took it as an opportunity to sightsee. On the drive to the restaurant, I looked out at beautiful parks with children playing while the parents watched from a nearby bench. I couldn't help but wonder if Ted and I could make a life for ourselves. Not that I wanted to have children. I was almost forty-two and was fairly certain that everything had dried up by now.

"Mae. You look gorgeous, as always." Ted took my hand in his and kissed it lightly.

I tried not to blush, but I couldn't control myself when I was near him. "Thank you. You look quite handsome, yourself."

At the restaurant, we took our seats across from one another and I surveyed the room. The restaurant was quaint, the kind that I wouldn't think twice about visiting often. It was small and, from the outside, appeared to be a hole in the wall. But once inside, the decor was fabulous with white linen tablecloths, lit candles in the center of every table, and soft, romantic music playing in the background. I could see why Ted enjoyed this place, though I found myself wondering who he'd brought here in the past.

"You have to try their ravioli." Ted tapped the menu. "The chef makes each one by hand, and they practically melt in your mouth."

I watched his mouth as he spoke and wanted to jump over the table and tackle him. That wouldn't be very ladylike, so I refrained. "That sounds delicious."

After we ordered, Ted reached across the table and held my hand. He was so romantic. "I'm so happy that you're feeling better. I couldn't stand seeing you in pain."

I squeezed his hand. "Me, too. Those headaches were no joke. Worst I've ever had."

"And how's Lela feeling?" Ted asked with concern in his eyes. His concern for her melted me. He knew that Lela, Harriet, and Bertha were the most important people in my life, and he embraced them with open arms.

"She's feeling more like herself, as well." I took a sip of water. "I didn't want her to suffer, but it's been much better today."

Ted laughed and leaned forward onto the table. "Sorry about my brother dropping in on our dinner the other night. I hope you didn't mind me asking him and Eleanor to join us."

"Oh, I don't mind at all." I crossed my legs and wondered if now might be a good time to ask about Joseph. "He and Eleanor were wonderful company. She's an absolute doll."

"Eleanor is the best." Ted smiled. "Try as I might, I can't keep myself from spoiling that little girl. She exudes so much happiness and innocence."

I nodded my head. "She seems to feel the same way about you. How long has she had her own bedroom at your house?"

"Oh, from the moment I heard that Joseph's wife didn't make it through the labor, I knew that I needed to step up and be there for him and Eleanor." He paused as if recalling the sad memory. "Adding a bedroom was an easy decision. Joseph needs a break every now and then, and I'm happy to be the fun uncle that lets Eleanor stay up too late and eat too much ice cream."

I giggled. Ted was too good to be true. "Lela was impressed with your brother."

"Oh, yeah?" Ted released my hand and sat back, crossing his arms. "Do tell."

"She'd kill me if she knew I was telling you this." I paused and wondered if I was betraying my sister's trust but pushed those thoughts away when I realized that this could be the match she's waited for her whole life. "Lela seemed to click with Eleanor. And I think she's attracted to Joseph."

A mischievous look spread across Ted's face. "Maybe we should have dinner at my house again and invite Lela, Joseph, *and* Eleanor."

I chuckled. "Sounds like a plan."

He smiled. "Let's do it then."

"What are the chances they'd end up together?" I wondered out loud. "Is Joseph even interested in dating? I'm sure he still struggles with the loss of his wife."

"Yeah, it's been rough on him." Ted's voice became sober. "After counseling and years of mourning, I think he's ready to get back out there. I don't think he should rush anything, of course."

"Definitely not." I didn't want Ted to think that I was forcing my sister and his brother into a relationship.

It couldn't hurt to talk about it, though. Right?

"I'll ask you a similar question. Do you think Lela would be ready for a committed relationship?" Ted paused and watched my face for a reaction. Apparently, we were interviewing each other about our siblings and their worthiness. "With a child involved, I wouldn't want Lela to consider Joseph a casual option. He needs someone who will be there for him and Eleanor for the long haul."

"That's true." I sighed. "From my point of view, I just want to make sure Lela doesn't get hurt again. But she definitely showed interest in Joseph and I know she wouldn't waste his time if she weren't interested, especially with Eleanor involved."

Ted nodded in agreement. "Well, it's all set. Lela is officially betrothed to Joseph."

We both laughed and enjoyed the rest of the evening. As usual, Ted had pointed out the yummiest menu item. After another hour of good food and conversation, Ted suggested I follow him back to his place for coffee, then insisted on following me back up the mountain. He worried about me driving in the dark on the curvy roads, and I didn't mind being doted over.

Ted turned his car engine off and came around to open my car door for me. He held my hand and walked with me to the front porch. "I enjoyed spending time with you tonight, Mae."

I turned to face Ted as he pulled me in close. My head fit perfectly into the crook of his neck, and I breathed in the scent of his cologne. "Me, too. Thank you for a wonderful evening."

Ted pulled away and looked deeply into my eyes. The old me tried to convince myself that I was falling too quickly for this man. Pushing those thoughts aside, I allowed his soft lips to brush against mine. Leaving all of my anxieties from my past relationship behind, I held Ted's head with both of my hands and kissed him deeply, allowing his hands to caress my neck and back. Lightning bolts shot through my body as Ted's strong arms held me tighter.

Finally, when we both knew it was time to go, Ted said goodbye. He drove away and the late summer breeze rustled my hair as I watched him disappear around the corner.

I found my key at the bottom of my purse and sighed deeply. Maybe I would find a happy ending after all.

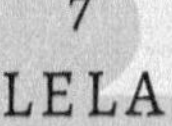

7

LELA

"It's nice of Ted to invite me to another dinner," I said as I put my earrings in. Mae was already ready of course. The woman hadn't been late a day in her life.

She didn't rush me, instead she just beamed. "He's a peach, isn't he?"

"How'd Harry's test go?" I asked and grabbed my purse.

"She did wonderfully! She's so smart, Lela." Mae smiled and lightly blushed. We both chuckled as we got into the car. Both of us knew darn well Harriet was more intelligent than both of us. She was our pride and joy. On the way to Ted's, Mae's phone rang.

"It's Bertha." She sighed and hit the speakerphone on the car. "Go ahead Bertha, what is it?"

"I've been threatened within an inch of my life not to show up tonight, I know, but I was wondering if Ted makes his famous mac and cheese, perhaps I could get a doggie bag?"

Mae made a sound, sort of like a moose, and picked up her phone. It was a pointless gesture since the call was going through the car's Bluetooth as I drove, but she still pulled the phone receiver nearer her mouth. "Bertha, you weren't supposed to mention that." Why would Bertha have been threatened? I had questions that Mae needed to answer when she hung up.

"Oh." Bertha didn't say anything for a moment. "Okay. Um, I'll talk to you later."

Our aunt hung up and Mae set her phone down. "Bertha's got the biggest mouth," she said, then shrugged. "I guess the secret is out."

"What secret?" I turned up the road to Ted's house and glanced at my sister. "Why is Bertha not allowed to come around specifically tonight?"

She blushed and looked very guilty. "Ted and I arranged for Joseph and Eleanor to come to dinner tonight as well."

My heart leaped in excitement. I really liked Joseph, and Eleanor had been wonderful. "Oh?" I tried so hard to sound casual. "So why was Bertha threatened?"

Mae sighed and bit her lip. "You know I love Bertha. I do. But if she found out we were trying to push you and Joseph together, she'd find a way to make it all..."

"Awkward?" I supplied an appropriate word.

"Yeah. Awkward," Mae said and nodded.

I grinned. I'd been trying to think of a way to get them to invite us all to dinner again but hadn't wanted to come out and say it. "Okay, well, then we're having dinner with Joseph and Eleanor."

Mae smiled and nodded. "Yes, we are."

We arrived at Ted's house, but Joseph hadn't arrived yet. I was a little relieved because I'd made myself up for a dinner with my sister and her boyfriend, not with a prospective suitor. As soon as I could delicately excuse myself, I headed to Ted's half bath and used what little bit of makeup I kept in my purse to plump up my mascara and turn my lipstick from clear gloss to a more dramatic red. I fluffed my hair and pinched my cheeks, then stared myself down in the mirror. My heterochromatic eyes blinked back at me. "You can do this," I whispered. "Don't be nervous."

My stomach's butterflies didn't listen to me one bit.

At least, not at first. The third time Ted called Joseph, half an hour later, the last butterfly left. "Did he know I was going to be here?" I asked.

"No. I was going to tell him right before, but he's not been responding. I'm actually a little worried." Ted dialed Joseph again, and again it went to voicemail.

Mae put her hand on Ted's arm. "If something's wrong, he'll call you. Let's eat and try to have a nice evening."

She gave me a sympathetic look. *He didn't even know you'd be here.*

I glared at my sister. *I know. Don't feel sorry for me.*

Even though I was feeling sorry for myself. I tried to put on a happy face, which was a little bit easier to do when Ted brought out his deep-fried macaroni and cheese. "Bertha's gonna be so mad."

Ted grinned. "I've got a big serving set aside in the kitchen for you ladies to take home for her." He winked at Mae. "And one for Harriet."

Mae leaned over and pressed a kiss to his cheek and then maybe I felt sorry for myself. I wanted that, too.

Halfway through the unusually quiet meal, Ted's phone rang. "It's a strange number."

He hit the speaker button. "Hello?"

"Ted, it's Joseph. I left my phone at home."

"What's wrong?" Ted went on alert, scooting his chair back and half-standing. Even I could hear the anguish in Joseph's voice. Something was definitely bad.

"It's Eleanor. We were just about to leave to come to your place. I was getting some stuff together for her to play with over there. She was on her swing. I called for her, but she didn't answer."

Joseph was silent for a second as Ted's face fell. "She fell off the swing," Joseph said in a strangled voice. Her little body was crumpled underneath it when I got out there."

"How is she now?" Ted asked in a low voice.

"We're at the hospital. She wouldn't wake up. She still hasn't. They've got her in one of those machines." His voice was shaky. "Uh, MRI, I think."

I stood and walked closer to the phone. "Joseph, this is Lela. Mae's sister."

"Oh, yes, hello."

"Do you know what Mae and I are?" There was no time to beat around the bush. "We're granny witches."

"Yes, I know. I'm familiar with the coven." The poor man. He sounded like he was about to lose his last grasp on his wits.

"I have the power to heal, Joseph. And I'm on my way, okay?"

By the time I finished the sentence, Ted had grabbed his cell and Mae had stood. We were out the door five seconds later, leaving dinner on the table. Ted only took enough time to make sure he'd turned the oven off.

"I'll drive," Mae said. "You're both too upset."

The county hospital was in the next town over, a larger town than Townsend. I'd been here to eat a few times and it was far too bustling for me. I preferred the quiet of the mountains, especially after living my life in L.A.

"We're lucky to have a hospital at all," Ted said nervously. "So many county hospitals have closed over the last several years." He rubbed his hands on his pants and jiggled one leg. "It's not got the best reputation, though."

"I've read about it," I said. "But it's a good sign that they didn't airlift her to Knoxville, right?"

Ted shrugged. "I don't know. They may be assessing her first."

"As long as we can get to her, I can take care of it." I nodded confidently. "No problem."

Ted kept looking at his phone, then groaned. "Ugh, he doesn't have his phone. I was going to text him when we were close." He pointed to the next road coming up. "Turn here."

"Go." Mae stopped the car by the emergency room doors, then turned to look at us. "I'll park then find you."

We jumped out of the car and rushed inside. "We're here for Eleanor Sullivan. I'm her uncle."

The nurse nodded. "She's just coming back from imaging, but it's only two visitors at a time."

"Her aunt will go in," he said, putting his hand on my back. "Eleanor will want to see her Aunt Lela."

The nurse, an older woman with kind eyes, smiled. "Come through those doors." She pressed a button and a set of double doors outside her kiosk opened. I hurried through them and met her on the other side. "Right this way."

She walked quickly, but I had no trouble keeping up. I could've sprinted there. We stopped outside a room where Joseph stood, looking from me to the interior of the room through the open door. "She's in there," the nurse said softly, nodding toward the door. "Let me know if you need anything."

I wanted to greet Joseph, but that wasn't what he needed. I pushed past him and into the room. "Shut the door."

Eleanor was hooked up to several machines. As a nurse and doula, I'd seen them all. One monitored her brain activity, one her heart. And the IV gave her fluids. I didn't stop to see what medicine they were putting in her. Soon it would be unnecessary. "You came just in time," Joseph whispered. "They're getting a helicopter to transfer her to Children's Hospital in Knoxville. The scan they did shows a bleed in her brain. They think she hit a rock under her swing."

I didn't reply, just put my hand on her head and drew on my power. I didn't want to slam it into her, so I let it trickle, flowing from me into the sweet little girl. With my other hand, I stroked her black hair and willed her to open her pretty gray eyes.

"Is it working?" Joseph whispered a minute later.

I didn't answer, but I did nod. I couldn't feel or tell exactly what my magic was doing, but I did get the sense that it was working.

"I should've put that mulch down under the swing set." He grabbed Eleanor's hand and a sob wracked him. It was distracting me a little. I wanted to comfort him, to tell him that it was going to be okay, but I had to stay focused on my healing.

Finally, what felt like hours later but was probably less than three minutes, Eleanor opened her eyes and smiled up at me. "Hello, Mae."

I opened my mouth to correct her, but it wasn't time for that. I moved out of the way as Joseph practically collapsed on top of his daughter, sobbing and pulling her into his arms.

Pulling out my phone, I texted Mae.

She's awake. Be out in a minute.

"I told Mae," I said once Joseph had calmed down enough to hear it. "She'll tell Ted."

A nurse stuck her head in the door a moment later, saw Eleanor awake, and then the room was swarmed. I snuck out, leaving Joseph and his daughter to deal with the doctors and hopefully get the helicopter canceled. He knew it was a magical healing. He'd have to figure out how to explain it. I needed to sit down, anyway. I'd done the healing slowly, but that had almost been harder than giving her the magic all at once. Like I'd used my muscles more or something. It made no sense.

"Lela, wait."

Joseph's deep, smooth voice calling to me down the hall sent shivers all over me.

He caught up to me and put his hand on my arm. "Thank you. I don't know how to thank you enough."

I shrugged, trying not to blush. "She's okay now," I said. "I'm really glad I could help."

He nodded and leaned in, his lips brushing against my forehead. "You are a miracle worker, Lela," he said softly.

I wanted to melt into him, but I stepped back. "I should get out of here, and you have to go play dumb and innocent about how she's all better now." I grinned. "I didn't heal her completely. She'll need rest and recovery, but as soon as you get her out of here, I'll get her back to as good as she was before she fell."

Joseph nodded and took my hand, squeezing it and looking deep into my eyes before turning and walking back towards his daughter's room. I watched him go, feeling like I was going to collapse from exhaustion.

Time to get to my sister. STAT.

8
MAE

"All right, Casper. I'm going to need you to stop making a fool out of me." I wagged my finger at the cauldron as I chastised the elusive ghost.

Since it was early evening on a Friday, Harriet hadn't arrived for the weekend yet. Bertha was at her house doing whatever crazy, old, mountain ladies did in their spare time. And Lela was getting her nails done, no doubt to impress a certain gentleman who now had a totally healthy little girl.

With everyone away, it was the perfect opportunity for me to try and conjure the ghost again. I got the sense that she wanted to tell me something, but every attempt to communicate had failed. I was missing something, but couldn't put my finger on it.

I knelt next to the cauldron and took a deep breath. Maybe there were special words I should chant? Or perhaps the room should be darker with candles burning? Quickly determining that I'd seen way too many horror movies, I moved my hands to the cauldron and gave it a good rub down.

Almost instantly, a fuzzy image appeared in the air behind the big, black pot. I gasped and clung to the cauldron in shock. "There you are!" I cried out, happiness bubbling up from within me.

The ghostly figure came into clearer view. She wore a big smile as she floated closer to me. "Hello again," she said with a gentle voice and thick, Scottish accent. My heart nearly leaped out of my chest when I heard her speak.

This time I could make out the red hue of her long hair. Her complexion was pale but she was certainly beautiful. She looked to be in her thirties or early forties. Such a young age to die.

"My name is Mae." I placed my hand on my chest and realized I had spoken very slowly as if she might not be able to understand me.

The ghost smiled and mimicked my gesture. "I'm Florie."

Florie. What an interesting name.

She floated toward the center of the kitchen, allowing me to see her full body. Her attire was not from modern times. There were so many periods in the past when women wore simple, long skirts and aprons that I couldn't figure out when she'd been alive.

"Do you know why you're here?" I asked, my voice trembling as the words escaped my lips. Florie didn't scare me, but her presence did. I had a bad feeling about whatever she might need from me.

Florie's expression softened, but before she could answer my question, she disappeared without warning.

Lela walked through the front door a moment later and dropped her keys on the side table. Glancing down at her hands, she sighed loudly. "I don't know why I haven't had my nails done since we moved to Tennessee. It always makes me feel so fancy."

I grunted loudly. "Lela! You scared Florie away."

"Who in the world is Florie?" Lela looked around the room and toward the door, trying to figure out who might be in the house without her knowledge.

"The ghost. She appeared to me again and this time told me her name." I stood from the floor and walked toward Lela, crossing my arms disapprovingly. "She was just about to tell me why she keeps appearing."

"Umm. Sorry?" Lela shrugged her shoulders and walked to the kitchen, opening the fridge to grab a drink. "I find it interesting that only you can see *Florie*, don't you?"

"As a matter of fact, Miss Smarty Pants, I think I've finally figured it out." I sat on a bar stool. "For some odd reason, she must be connected to me and my magic. If Florie can only appear to me, that would explain her disappearing anytime someone else comes into the room."

Lela stared at me and nodded her head. I couldn't tell if she believed me or if she still thought this was all a prank. I didn't care. I was determined to figure out why Florie had come back from beyond the dead, and what she wanted from me.

Placing my hands on my hips, I walked toward Lela. "Now that you've got what you needed, why don't you head to your bedroom and close the door?"

"Why?" Lela was confused at my request and looked at me as if I had two heads.

"You know why." I rolled my eyes. "I'm going to try and bring Florie back and you can't be around, or you'll scare her off."

"Sorry to be the bearer of bad news, Mae." Lela tapped her smartwatch. "We have to leave in five minutes for the coven meeting."

"Poop." I stomped my foot like a toddler. "I forgot all about that."

"How could you forget?" Lela sat her soda can on the kitchen counter. "This is our chance to share our magic with the coven."

I was surprised that I'd forgotten about the meeting, especially since I'd been reading the grimoire over and over again in an attempt to fully understand the spell. Turning to face the cauldron, I shrugged. "Until next time, Florie."

Lela patted my back. "Yes. Florie will have to wait until later to play with you, Mae."

She didn't even try to hide her laughter as I gathered my purse, phone, and the grimoire. I had to find a way to make Florie feel safe around my family and soon before Lela decided to talk to Ted about my mental instability.

WHEN WE WALKED into the coven meeting, I scanned the room for Ted. He'd become my anchor at these meetings. No matter what was being discussed, it was over-the-top interesting simply because Ted was seated by my side.

He'd spotted me first and was already a few feet from me when Bertha hollered my name. She was standing by the refreshment table, as usual.

"Hello, beautiful," Ted whispered in my ear, sending a chill down my neck.

I held a finger up. "Hold that thought. Bertha needs my attention for a moment."

Ted kissed me gently on the cheek. "Don't be long."

Good grief, we were disgusting. As I walked to Bertha, I glanced around the room to make sure no one had noticed Ted's sweet words. They made my heart flutter but I could only imagine how sickening it could be for some of the other coven members. Or my sister.

"Bertha, did you need something?" I reached for a cookie and took a small bite.

"Yes, darlin'. I wanted to remind you to talk to Constance about our plans for this meeting." Bertha nodded in our leader's direction. "She can get a little annoyed when people don't let her know the topics to be discussed ahead of time. You know, agendas and such."

"Right." I liked Constance, and I was in awe of her ability to run a business and coordinate all of the coven activities and meetings. Yet there was still something about her that rubbed me the wrong way. Maybe it was the fact that she was best friends with the woman who'd tried to kill Bertha.

Rubbing my head, I realized that my headache had come back. It wasn't as intense as it had been, but passing some of our magic on to coven members was definitely a necessity.

I smiled at Bertha and made my way over to Constance, who was furiously writing something in her handy, dandy notebook.

Clearing my throat, I gently placed my hand on her shoulder.

Constance jumped with surprise and then laughed. "Oh, Mae. I didn't see you there. How are you today?"

"I'm doing well, thank you." Ted walked past us, and I was distracted by the faint smell of his cologne, not to mention watching him walk away. Whew. That man had a nice tush.

"I wanted to let you know that Lela and I would like to try out a spell this evening." I glanced at Constance who now gave me her full attention.

She placed her notebook on the table and crossed her arms. "Is that so? What kind of spell?"

"It's a long story, but Lela and I have been getting physically ill from the buildup of all the mountain magic within us. We'd like to try and share some of those powers." I paused and waited for Constance's response. "Of course, we'll ask for volunteers."

"I see." She bit her fingernail nervously. "If you think it will help you and Lela, that sounds like a good plan. We'll just have to hope that there are no...snafus."

Snafus? What did she think this was? An episode of Scooby Doo? We were powerful granny witches with ancient spells at our fingertips. Surely nothing would go wrong.

"Yep. Hopefully, it will go smoothly." I turned and walked toward Ted before Constance could respond. I wasn't in the mood to get into a useless argument.

Lela had already found a seat near Leon, though I doubted that was her choice. He seemed to have a thing for Lela and tended to follow her around the meetings like a lost puppy dog. I hadn't specifically talked to her about it, but it was painfully obvious he made her uncomfortable.

"If I could have everyone's attention, please." Constance made her way to the head of the room. "We have a special request from Mae and Lela this evening, so I'm going to turn the meeting over to them."

The room applauded as my cheeks reddened. I hadn't expected it to be such a production. Lela joined me in the front of the room and nodded in my direction, giving me the go-ahead.

"Hello, everyone." I smiled at the crowd. "As some of you know, Lela and I haven't been feeling well lately. We thought maybe we'd caught a virus, but the symptoms never subsided. After visiting someone with a lot of knowledge on granny witches, we realized that we've accumulated too much magic within our bodies and it was making us physically ill."

The faces staring back at us grew concerned. They'd become like family to us, and for that, I was eternally grateful. We'd started this journey with no family and now we had a multitude of people who had our backs.

Harriet walked in through the door and waved. She'd texted earlier saying that she hoped to make it to the meeting but the traffic in Knoxville was horrendous.

Lela cleared her throat. "We have a request, but please, don't feel obligated to volunteer. If there's anyone who'd like to take some of the magic that is overwhelming us, we have a spell that should allow us to share with others."

The crowd murmured and discussed the option with one another.

"Just to be clear," I added, "we're not exactly sure what the magic-sharing will entail. Your existing powers might increase or you might end up with new abilities."

Lela nodded in agreement. "Yes, so please don't volunteer if you already feel overwhelmed with your current level of magical abilities."

"And," I said, "we're more than willing to let men attempt this. Perhaps you'll gain powers, perhaps not, but any who would like to try are welcome."

That caused a bit of a stir, and within seconds, several volunteers made their way to the front of the room, including Harriet, Bertha, Ted, George, and Leon. As if the situation wasn't already anxiety-inducing, Leon had to take it up a notch. He kept winking awkwardly at Lela. That poor man didn't know how to flirt.

"Okay, let's get started." I pulled the grimoire from my purse and opened it to the page I had book-marked. "If everyone would please stand over here." I pointed to the left side of the room.

Lela and I took our positions standing directly across from the group so that we were facing one another. I raised one hand and repeated the words that had been written by Susan several decades ago. Most made no sense, but I didn't question them.

Once I read the final words of the spell, a purple mist appeared and surrounded Lela and me. It swirled faster and faster until we no longer could see the group of volunteers. The mist was cool and refreshing and caused a slight tingle in my hands and feet. After a few seconds, though, the mist shifted from us and drifted over to the volunteers who stood, mesmerized, as it encircled them.

Just as quickly as the mist had appeared, it rose to the ceiling and disintegrated.

The volunteers looked down at their hands, rubbed their arms, and whispered amongst themselves. I turned to Lela. My mind was clear and there wasn't a pain in my body, especially my head. "I feel fantastic. How about you?"

Lela thought for a moment before a huge grin spread across her face. "Yes, it's like a weight's been lifted. It must've worked."

We turned to the volunteers, who were already trying out their new abilities. To our shock, the men now had abilities. It had worked.

After the women of the coven surrounded the men and helped them figure out their new magic, we determined that Ted could create fire with a snap of his finger. George knew the answer to any question asked of him, giving him an ego boost, which Lela whispered privately he certainly didn't need.

Most surprisingly of all, Leon was able to fly. Well, more like levitate. And he kept crashing into the ceiling, which was a bit comical. Okay, it was a lot comical.

For the first time in history, there were now male granny witches.

Bertha and Harriet said that they didn't notice anything new, but I instinctively knew that they wanted to try out their abilities in the privacy of our mountain property.

The room erupted in applause and cheers as we all celebrated the successful spell. Lela and I had succeeded in transferring our magic and, hopefully, wouldn't become physically ill from excess energy ever again.

The rest of the coven meeting was spent helping the men harness their powers and learn how to control them. The other volunteers had various abilities, some even included plant power and animal communication. No one, however, had received the ability to manipulate water or heal.

Lela turned to Constance, who had watched quietly all night from the corner. "Looks like we have an even more powerful coven, now."

"Yes." Constance crossed her arms. "Hopefully the spell will hold."

There was that enthusiasm and positive thinking. Perhaps she was still holding out for a good 'ol snafu.

9

LELA

"I don't know, Mae. If you were going to be picky about them, you should've come yourself. Or ordered it online." I looked from the cream-colored outlet covers to the white. "Pick a color."

She hemmed and hawed for a second before saying, "Uuummmmm, white!" Finally. I hung up the phone and counted out light switch covers, put them in my little handbasket, and then counted out outlet covers. They had just enough. Score.

"Hey, there, Lela."

Oh, no. I knew that voice. Leon. It wasn't that I minded running into him, but the last time we were together at the coven meeting, he was so awkward.

"Hey, Leon." I turned and plastered a smile on my face.

He had on a tight-fitting navy blue shirt and a pair of jeans that hung off his hips just so, making my heart flutter a little bit. If I was being honest, he was quite attractive—but not as attractive as Joseph. And Joseph made me feel all the warm fuzzies, not just a little fluttered at his hotness. Too bad Joseph hadn't contacted me at all since the hospital. It was understandable, considering what he'd been through, but shoot. A text might've been nice. He could've gotten my number from Ted.

Maybe he didn't feel the same fuzzies I did. That was okay. I'd be fine.

"What are you up to?" Leon asked, leaning against the wall and crossing his arms.

"Oh, just grabbing these outlet covers for the new house." I held up the little handbasket.

After peeking down into the basket, he nodded toward the switches. "You went with white, huh?" As he spoke, he reached over and squeezed my arm. I didn't particularly like it, but who else was trying to flirt with me?

"Yeah, I think it will look better with the tan walls than cream." Now that I was saying it, I realized how much more attractive the white switches would be. Why was buying switches such an important decision? Ugh, was this middle age?

"You've got a good eye," he said, dropping his hand to his side.

I nodded and looked away, not wanting to encourage his advances. He had a good heart, but I just wasn't interested in him, not really. "Thanks. Renovating the house has been kind of amazing. It was great you were there to make the process easier on us, considering we're..." I looked around to make sure nobody was in earshot. "Witches and all."

He nodded. "Cool. I was glad to do it." He leaned in a teeny bit closer. "Hey, do you want to go get coffee or something?"

I froze for a second, and then I shook my head. "No, thanks. I'm all set."

I didn't want to hurt Leon's feelings or anything, but Joseph was the only one who had been on my mind lately and until I heard from him again, no other man was going to get any of my attention.

"Okay," he said, but then looked down at his feet. "I mean, just as friends. I miss hanging out with you ladies." He chuckled and stepped back a little. "We got to be friends there for a while."

Maybe I was reading too much into his words and actions. He'd been standing a little close, sure, but maybe he just wanted to be friends.

"Friends it is," I said, nodding. "I'd love a cup of coffee, friend."

He grinned big. "Okay, I'll go grab the socket I needed and meet you across the street at Cross Creek Coffee."

I nodded, then grabbed the screwdriver we still needed before paying. Ten minutes later, I smiled at a perky, young barista. "Iced coffee with mocha, please." It was a little late in the day to be drinking coffee, but oh, well.

Leon walked in and gave me a shy smile. "Hey, stranger."

"Hello." This wasn't awkward at all. "I got us a table over there." I nodded toward the front window. It was the only table open. This place was popular. It had been every time I'd stopped in for a muffin or coffee.

We sat and I tried to look anywhere but at Leon as he ordered.

"So," he said after a long, silent minute. "How's Mae?"

It was a good thing we kept our hair and styles totally different. I didn't miss being mistaken for my sister like we had when we were young. "She's good. She's out today with Harriet and Bertha."

The barista walked over with our drinks. I accepted the iced coffee and thanked her.

Leon took his cup in both hands and then looked at me with a smile. "How's Bertha doing? She's such a character."

I laughed. "She's doing well, thanks for asking. She's still as feisty as ever."

He nodded and took a sip from his cup. "That's great, I'm glad to hear it."

We sat and sipped for a few minutes before Leon continued, "And Harriet? How are her college classes going?"

"Well. She had such a good first test that she talked Mae into taking her shopping for updates to her winter wardrobe. That's where they are today. Bertha tagged along, of course."

Leon smiled and nodded. "Good for Harriet. She was a good helper to us this summer. Saved you a few dollars in labor, too."

A few seconds later, he said, "So, tell me about your family. I know they've lived in the area for a long time, but I don't know much about your history. I mean, I know you didn't know your grandmother before she passed, but nothing specific."

That seemed a little personal, but perhaps not for another Appalachian native. He likely had family from the area as well and was being politely curious. "Well, it's rather complicated." I chuckled and sucked in a deep breath to try to make it all make sense. "My grandmother, Susan, was born a Sparks. But she married Thomas Myers. The house we renovated was the Myers family home."

He nodded. "Right, right, I recall that mentioned."

"Bertha never married, and she lives on the old Sparks family homestead, though I think her cabin is the second one on the land."

He opened his mouth to comment, but I kept going. Rude? Maybe. But I was on a roll. "My mom and aunt were twins. Eliza Jane, who we called Aunt EJ, and my mother was Lela Mae, hence our names."

He chuckled. "What is with Appalachians reusing names? If you dig farther back into your family history, I'd bet you'll find a lot of names trickling down through generations."

I nodded and pointed at him. "I've done a tiny bit of research and already found that to be true." I'd barely scratched the surface, and it had been back before we'd started this family history journey. I'd mostly looked at my father's side of things back then. Who knew my mother's side would be so much more interesting?

"Mae and I were raised by Aunt EJ, but our father was a Cable. I know there is a lot of Cable history here in the area, but we haven't dug into it yet."

"I'd love to see the old house again." One corner of Leon's mouth curled up. "Maybe for dinner sometime?"

"Sure, we can do that sometime." For some reason, I was reluctant to invite him. He'd been perfectly pleasant and he'd built most of the house. There was no reason not to have him over, and yet...

He moved on and said, "Back to the Myers." He sipped his coffee and looked at me expectantly when I didn't answer. "They lived in that old house, on that land?"

"Bertha says she's pretty sure the house dates back to the early twentieth century, but I think there must've been homes before that because the Myers's have been here for a long time. She said the outhouse was two-hundred years old." I wasn't exactly sure how long our family had owned the property.

"How long?" He leaned forward and rested his chin on his hand. Of course, he asked that. What was his obsession with my family all of a sudden?

"At least two hundred years, maybe longer." I shrugged. "We just don't know for sure yet. We haven't had time to really dig into researching our family tree."

"Interesting, interesting. Do you know which of your ancestors were also..." He glanced around and must've thought the room was too crowded. "Like you and Mae? Special?"

I winked, catching his drift. "Not a clue. We—" I cut off, the realization dawning on me. "We've never asked if the Cables had our special, er, traits."

Leon winked back at me. Shoot. Probably shouldn't have done that. "Might be worth looking into."

I nodded and smiled, my mind racing with possibilities. We already knew it was possible we had more family somewhere out there but were they witches?

"I'm sorry to cut this short, Leon, but I need to go talk to my sister."

He waved his hand at me. "Shoot, we're friends, remember? No sweat." He stood as I gathered my trash and purse.

Before I pulled out of the parking lot, I dialed Mae. She answered on the first ring. "Chello?"

"Hey, sis, is Bertha with you?"

"You got me, babe." Oh, good, I was on speaker.

"Bertha, tell me about the Cables. Were they magical?"

"Well, sure. But they aren't nary a one of them left. Poor Robert was the last of that clan. There may be some distant cousins, but as far as Susan knew, all of Robert's kin were gone."

I sighed in disappointment. "Oh, well. I was hoping you'd have bigger news for us."

"Sorry to disappoint you, Sweets. It's just us as far as family goes."

"Is there some sort of Cable family land?" Mae asked. "Could we have any history with the family?"

Bertha hummed for a second. "I don't know. Susan would've taken care of it, I suppose." She made some sort of clapping sound. Knowing her she literally clapped. "I'll look into it."

"I'm headed home." I regaled them on the drive with the story of Leon and his interest in our family history.

"Lela," Mae said flatly. "Did you even ask him about his new powers? How they're working?"

His powers! Of course. That's why he was interested. He'd always been a granny witch but had never had the magic. Now he had magic and I hadn't even bothered to ask. I was a total rat. "I'm home, talk to you later!"

I hung up before Mae could give me a lecture about being a bad friend. I had a good excuse for hanging up, though. There was something waiting on the front porch.

A giant bouquet of wildflowers. It wasn't something from a florist. This looked like they'd been plucked straight from a summer field. And it was late in the season to be finding flowers like this.

"Oh," I whispered as I picked up a hand-drawn card. On one side, a child had drawn a little stick figure with a bandage on her head. The words *thank you* were scrawled underneath. Little Eleanor was only four, so that was a big accomplishment for the sweet little girl.

On the other side of the card was a message.

Lela,

I can't thank you enough for helping Eleanor. Your healing touch is a gift. We will forever be in your debt. If you ever need a friend, we're here.

Sincerely,

Joseph

My heart warmed and I clutched the flowers close. Joseph. He hadn't forgotten me. If I hadn't been on that stupid coffee *date* with Leon, I would've been here when Joseph came by.

As soon as I got in the house, I pulled my phone out and opened a text to Joseph. We'd exchanged numbers after leaving the hospital. **Thank you for my flowers. They're beautiful. I'm still more than willing to stop by and do another healing on sweet Eleanor, to get her up to snuff.**

After sending that, I considered my options. **We never got our dinner the other night. Would you like to come over for dinner?**

His reply shot back as though he'd just been sitting and waiting for it, which I prayed he had been. **I'd love to. She's doing very well, actually. So well, I didn't think further healing was necessary, though I thank you for the offer.**

Oh, good. I was so glad. I'd healed her better than I'd thought. **Next weekend?** That gave him a whole week and me a week to make sure I was prepared for it.

He replied that it was perfect, so I told him to please bring Eleanor.

It was a date. With Joseph.

Holy shmow.

10

MAE

THIS MAGIC SURE COMES IN HANDY. I USED IT THIS morning to burn a pile of leaves in my backyard.

Giggling, I responded to Ted's text.

I expect a warm fire in your fireplace every time I visit.

It'd been two days since the men in the coven had received magical abilities, and Ted hadn't stopped acting like a kid on Christmas morning. He wasn't simply excited to create fire out of thin air. He'd admitted that he felt closer to me in some way. We now shared a rare bond, both of us extraordinarily tied to the mountains.

Sally peeped over the edge of her habitat and licked her lips. Do salamanders have lips? Either way, I could tell she was hungry, so I opened a bag of dried mealworms and scooped a spoonful into her tiny bowl.

Whenever possible, I took Sally out into the woods and let her roam and eat live insects. Sometimes it just wasn't feasible to get her outside for mealtime, so the local pet store had been a lifesaver.

Sally turned her nose into the air and sniffed at the smell of chicken wafting from the kitchen. Bertha had insisted on making Sunday dinner for us, and I hadn't dared tell her no. Her fried chicken was amazing, not to mention the mashed potatoes and gravy and homemade green beans she typically made as sides.

"I forgot my special seasoning." Bertha made her way into the living room. "The chicken's done, just leave it alone on the counter. I'll be back in just a bit."

I nodded and waved as she walked out the front door.

The cauldron caught my eye. I hadn't tried to summon Florie for a few days. Lela was in the shower and Harriet was working on a school assignment in the camper, so this was as good a time as any. It was rare for me to be in the living room alone.

Sally eyed me as if she could read my thoughts.

"Don't worry, Sally. You can stay." I rubbed her smooth back with one finger. "Florie doesn't seem to mind when you're nearby." Hopefully, I'd finally get some answers.

I made my way to the cauldron and rubbed the side as if my life depended on it. Bertha would be back soon and Lela's shower had been running for at least twenty minutes. That didn't mean much, though, as she tended to stay in long enough to have a nice lobster-like glow from the scalding hot water.

The air turned cold and a mist rose out of the cauldron. Florie appeared and looked around as if making sure there was no one else in the room.

I didn't waste any time. "Why can you only appear to me?"

"I'm drawn to your powers; they give me the energy to appear. The more folk in the room, the harder it is for me to be seen." Florie smoothed her apron.

"When anyone else is here, it's too muddled for me to find just your magic."

So it wasn't that she only wanted to appear to me. She was using my powers to manifest in front of the living. I hadn't thought about how difficult it must be to move from one realm to another. It made perfect sense.

"What if I pushed more energy to you?" I asked. "Would that allow you to stay formed when someone else is present?"

Florie looked off into the distance in deep thought. "It just might. We'll have to try it and see."

I couldn't help but smile. It felt like we were on the verge of a breakthrough in our odd granny witch and ghost relationship.

As if she'd overheard my conversation with Florie, Lela appeared in the kitchen with a towel wrapped around her hair. Florie disappeared just as Lela caught me sitting crisscross applesauce in front of the cauldron.

"Whatcha doing there, Mae?" Lela's voice was suspicious. She still didn't really believe all this.

"Hear me out, Lela." I stood and walked to the kitchen counter. "Florie appeared again, and she explained why she can't manifest when others are around."

"Right." Lela crossed her arms. "Of course she did." Ohh, I was gonna give my sister a good thump.

"I'm serious, Lela. This isn't a joke." I walked back over to the cauldron and pointed down at it. "If you'll come over here, I'll attempt to prove it to you."

"Fine." Lela threw her hands in the air. "But after this, I don't want to hear about the ghost again. It's getting old. Got it?"

I stood at attention and saluted my annoyed sister. "Yes, ma'am."

As soon as I rubbed the cauldron, I closed my eyes and focused my powers on the cauldron. The temperature changed and I glanced at Lela as she rubbed her arms and looked around suspiciously. Within seconds, Florie's profile began to form.

"What in the precious name of Goldie Hawn is that?" Lela stood and backed away from Florie.

An excited peep escaped my throat. "It's working, Florie." I tried harder to funnel power her way.

The ghost looked down at her hands and then back at me. "Wonderful." She turned her attention to Lela and floated toward my twin, who was now hunkered against the wall, unable to get any further from the apparition.

"You must be Mae's kin." Florie put her hand to her chest. "I'm Florie." Her lyrical Scottish accent was beautiful, even if it did make it slightly harder to understand her.

Lela opened her mouth to respond but all she managed to get out was a few grunts and a small whimper.

I ran to Lela's side and helped her up off of the ground. "It's okay, Lela. Florie's not going to hurt you."

"What does she w-want from us?" Lela stuttered, not taking her eyes off the floating ghost in the middle of our ancestral house. She wasn't normally this scared. Ghosts weren't Lela's thing. Important to note.

"That's an excellent question." I turned to Florie. "I'm assuming you have some sort of message for us? Or maybe a mystery that needs solving? Perhaps related to your death?"

Again, I'd watched far too many movies.

"I'm here to warn you." Florie's lips turned down and her eyes were fixated on us.

I didn't like the sound of a warning. Why couldn't she just say that she wanted to tell us that we were doing a fantastic job with the mountain magic? I thrived on positive feedback. A warning, though? Nah. Not interested.

"Warn us about what?" Lela grabbed my hand and squeezed until the circulation cut off. My fingers were gonna turn purple.

"No matter what happens, or how bad things might be, please lassies, please, don't *ever* use the golden coins." Florie raised her hands for emphasis. "Ever."

Lela and I looked at each other. We remembered the warning we'd received when we'd dug the coins up for the first time. The temperature had changed dramatically and ghostly voices forbade us from using the coins. The soft, green glow had been a nice touch. Definitely enough to make us heed the warning. Voices were one thing, but an actual ghost was a different story.

"Why can't we use them?" I pulled Lela closer to Florie. I wanted to stand next to her in case she needed more of my magic.

Florie floated upward until she hovered a few feet above the floor. "You must guard the coins with your life. If you spend them, you'll be cursed for eternity. And anyone else who spends them will result in you being cursed. They're in your care and you've been handed the responsibility of protecting them."

I shuddered. Seeing as how I had no interest in being cursed for eternity, I made a mental note to never use the coins. "You have nothing to worry about. We hid the coins and had no intention of cashing them in."

"I didn't believe in the curse when I was alive, so I spent some of them. The curse is very real, as you can see." Florie gestured to her transparent body.

So if you used the coins, you became a ghost, cursed to an object, for eternity. Noted.

"What was your connection to the coins?" The color had slowly returned to Lela's face and she seemed interested in what Florie had to say.

"The original twin witches, Agnes and Margaret, cursed the coins. I do not know how or why because I never paid mind to family lore." Florie shook her head. "If only I'd shown some interest in my kin's heritage, I wouldn't be in this cursed state."

Poor Florie. I wasn't sure if ghosts could cry, but if they could, she was certainly on the verge of a good cry.

"You said that you weren't sure exactly what happened with the coins being cursed." Lela loosened her grip on my hand but still held tight. "Is there some type of documentation we might be able to find?"

"There may have been, hundreds of years ago when I was alive, but I don't know where it would be." Florie's voice lowered. "Or if it even exists."

"We've been through everything on this property that we're aware of." I gestured toward our hiding hole in the wall. "And we've not seen any kind of written history or genealogy information."

Florie clasped her hands in front of her apron. "I was one of the first folk to migrate from Scotland to the United States. I used the coins to fund my journey."

"Wait." Lela pushed a strand of hair behind her ear. "Was it your voice we heard when we found the coins in the backyard?"

"Aye, I suppose." Florie picked at her fingernails, which were barely visible to me. "In my last few moments, I remember thinking that I'd like to warn others so they don't suffer the same fate. Perhaps those thoughts passed to the coins."

"Or maybe it was the twin witches you mentioned," I pointed out. "What were their names again?"

"Agnes and Margaret." Florie folded her arms across her chest. "They were extremely powerful witches. The first."

"Do you think they cursed anyone else besides you?" Lela leaned forward.

"I'm not sure." Florie's face was hard to read because it didn't show much emotion. "But I do know that if the coins are used, the curse will follow."

We all stood in silence for a few moments until Bertha burst through the door holding her jar of spices. Florie disappeared while Lela and I were left holding hands, looking stunned and confused, wondering exactly how Florie was tied to the cauldron and coins.

"Sorry I took so long." Bertha placed her keys and purse on the side table without looking up. "I had to drop a couple of kids off at the pool, if you know what I mean."

Bertha's sense of humor didn't faze us this time.

"Girls?" Bertha walked slowly toward us. "What did I miss? You look like you've seen a ghost."

"I don't know about you two, but I want to lay eyes on those coins." Bertha took her spices over to the counter. "Care to get them out?"

We'd recounted everything Florie had said to our aunt while she'd stared, wide-eyed. "I've heard of Florie and Alden Sparks. She was the first of our kin to move to America. Alden died fightin' the redcoats in the Revolutionary War."

I tried not to giggle at Bertha's serious tone. "What about Florie?" I asked. "Know anything about her?"

"It was a Scottish belief that the woman keeps her surname, but once Florie moved to America and married a Brit, she went with his traditions and took his name, instead."

"That's interesting." I wondered what else Florie had compromised on. "Can you tell me more about her life here in America?"

Bertha shook her head. "The records don't give women as much detail. She's buried in the old Sparks' family plot, I'm sure."

There was some information in the grimoire, but it was only a few generations old. Anything older had been lost to time.

This old woman sure was discerning about what information she gave us and when. "Family plot?" I prodded.

She started mashing the potatoes. "Sure. it's on the edge of my property, not too far from my house."

It was getting a little too dark outside to go look for it now, but that was something we'd definitely have to do.

Mae and I exchanged a look. Electric anticipation buzzed between us both.

"Let's go see if we can get any more information off of those coins." She winked at me, and I jumped up. Heck, I was eager to see them again myself. While

Mae stopped to tie her shoe, I walked into the kitchen.

Somewhere, somehow, I stumbled over my own two feet and launched forward. "No," I yelled, throwing my hand out in front of me. I managed to get one of my feet straightened and put my weight on it, but my left hand sank deep into the full garbage can. An intense, burning cramp ricocheted up my middle finger and I squealed in pain.

Mae and Bertha were at my side in a second, grabbing my arm to steady me. "What did you do?" Mae asked.

"I don't know." Blood poured out of the tip of my finger and down my hand. I'd cut the tip of my finger. Pretty deeply, by the looks and feel of it. "Oh, man, this stings." I rushed toward the sink before the blood dripped on the floor.

"Ow!" Mae yelled as Bertha hissed and grabbed her hand. Blood was dripping pretty steadily down their hands as well, especially Bertha's. She took a blood thinner, which would make sense that she'd bleed more.

The three of us crowded together at the sink, talking over one another and each of us trying to rinse our fingers. "Okay, I'm the one who actually came in contact with garbage," I said loudly.

"Good point." Mae wrapped her finger in a paper towel. "I'm going to get the first aid kit, then we're going to see what in the world is going on." She hurried away while Bertha wrapped her finger up in another paper towel. I waited for Mae to return with the peroxide. There was no telling what cut me in that garbage can, but I didn't want the bacteria moving all around me and making me sick. Blech.

It didn't occur to me until the peroxide was bubbling on my finger that if I did get sick, Mae could put on the ring and heal me, but then, this whole witch thing was still so new. It was easy to forget. "Hey, let me try to heal you." Bertha uncovered her cut, which immediately began to seep blood.

As quickly as I could, I covered her hand with mine and let my power flow through my hand and into hers while Mae put a small bandage on mine.

"Me next," Mae chirped. I didn't even cut off the flow of my power, just transferred it to Mae, and her finger healed up in a jiffy. "I'll grab the rings," Mae peered down at my finger, "I'll heal you, then we need to figure out why this happened."

We'd put the rings in her jewelry box and basi-cally forgotten about them. We hardly ever used them.

"Here you go." She handed me one of the rings, and then I held up my hand for her to attempt healing. She was much slower and clumsier at it than I was, but she rarely used it, so it was to be expected. A minute later, my finger healed up and the throbbing pain disappeared. I breathed a sigh of relief. "Oh, thank you."

Harriet burst into the room. "Mom, something weird is..." She stopped short and stared at her hand. "Um, weird."

"What?" Mae hurried over, but I had a sneaking suspicion I knew what was going on. It was all coming together.

"Is it her finger?" I asked.

Harriet looked over Mae's shoulder. "Yeah. I was just studying and all of a sudden, I had this horrible pain, and my finger just started spurting blood. It was like a horror movie. I'd just gotten it stopped and was on my way here to ask if magic can do such a crazy thing, and now it's all healed up. Gone." She huffed and looked almost cross-eyed at her middle finger.

In doing so, she was inadvertently flipping us all the bird.

"Okay, Harry, that's enough." Mae pulled her finger down and chuckled. "Something weird is going on."

"I think it's the bond." I held up my healed finger. "I bet if we called the others, they had the same thing happen."

As if on cue, Mae's phone rang. She stepped over to the kitchen table and smirked. "Yep. It's Ted."

Ted had taken some of our power, along with several others. "Hello?"

I was trying to listen to her side of the conversation, but then my phone pinged. I pulled it out of my back pocket to find a text from George, the nurse I'd sorta kinda almost dated.

Hey, Lela. Have you ever heard of small wounds appearing and disappearing? Or has Bertha?

"It happened to George, too," I called.

Instead of replying to him, I opened the coven's group chat and sent a message to all of them.

Emergency coven meeting at our house. Anybody who took our power or who is just interested in it. Get here ASAP please.

Mae squawked. "Ted, I gotta go." She glared at me. "We could've tried to have it at Constance's."

"Why?" I raised my eyebrows at her.

"It's a mess in here." She slung her phone onto the table, then rummaged around under the sink until she reemerged with a spray bottle of cleaner and a dust rag. To my dismay, she shoved them into my hands.

I wasn't the only one *volun-told* to clean. Soon she had Bertha putting up the food and cleaning the kitchen, *without* any of us being able to eat first. Harriet was in charge of sweeping and mopping the living room, entryway, and kitchen.

I had to hand it to my sister, she had a way of getting things done quickly. We finished the cleaning just in time for everyone to arrive, and it did look pretty good.

They all looked as if they didn't know what to expect. Mae had them sit in the living room and gave a quick rundown of our day. I took over after that, explaining how I'd been injured and then subsequently healed. Everyone had a similar story. They were doing nothing, but then their fingers opened up, bled, then a few minutes later, healed perfectly.

"Here's the grimoire," Bertha said, appearing from deeper in the house. Mae had asked her to put it away. "I think I know what's going on."

We all crowded around the grimoire, and Bertha pointed to the old spell we'd done. "The wording on this is a little ambiguous. We think when we did the spell, it linked us all physically as well as magically. But I have good news. There's a spell to unlink." She carefully turned the page. "It was stuck together."

George nodded at Mae. "Did your finger cut, too? You two didn't link to each other, just us."

Mae nodded as she inspected her now-healed finger. "Yes, but the spell must've given us a physical link since we already had a magical one." She shrugged. "Who knows at this point? This magic stuff feels like shuffling around in the dark half the time."

"Okay, so we unlink, then look for another solution." But my heart was heavy. This had seemed like the best option. Who knew what we would have to do now?

The unlinking spell was pretty much just like the linking, with the swirling purple mist and the tingling, but boy what a rush of power at the end. It was quite literally overwhelming.

Nausea slammed into me like a Mac truck with no brakes. It took me to my knees as Harriet and Ted rushed forward. Harriet grabbed my arm and Ted got Mae. George and Bertha helped. Each supported half my weight as I vomited thanks to the power I'd taken.

"Yuck." Mae waved one hand while the other clutched her right temple. My vomit rose from the floor like a floating mass of ewwwww. "Someone open the door, please."

Constance rushed forward and turned her head as the ick floated past her and out the door.

"Come on, girls." Bertha tugged on Mae and George guided me out the door and down the porch steps. I just saw the vomit disappear into the woods. "Now." Bertha spread her hands out. "Use your magic."

She had a good point. I blasted my magic out as hard as I could, manipulating the temperature in the area and calling all sick and injured animals to me.

They came pouring out of the woods within seconds. A few at a time, then more and more. As quickly as I could, I healed each one and sent them on their way.

After a few hours of healing, the house and yard were empty again. Everyone had left while we'd worked. I hadn't paid a lot of attention to what Mae was doing, but the ground was absolutely soaked now, and we had a couple of new trees beside the house. Thankfully, there was a nice bright moon to see it by, because it had gotten late.

"I'm going to bed," I muttered. Now that the nausea was gone, I was utterly exhausted, like the last time we'd done this. I pressed a kiss to Harriet's head. "Go. We're fine."

"Okay. Thanks, Aunt Lele. I would stay, but I have a class at eight in the morning."

Mae trudged up the walk and onto the porch. "Your aunt is right. Get back to your dorm before it gets too late." She gave her a kiss and walked past me into the house like a zombie. "Goodnight."

"Take Bertha home," I said weakly. "Please."

"Of course. You both go to bed." Harriet shook her head and took Bertha's arm. "Come on. Let's leave these two to their snore fests."

"Yeah, yeah." Bertha walked around Harry's car. "I need a nip anyway."

Mae was already in the house, but I had just enough strength to wave until Harriet and Bertha disappeared down the curve of the driveway. With a massive yawn, I shuffled straight to my bed, pointedly ignoring all the food Bertha had cooked for us. No way I could handle that now. I collapsed onto my bedspread without even washing my face.

Lights. Out.

12

MAE

A KNOCK AT THE DOOR STABBED LIKE DAGGERS through my temples. The headache that'd hit me after our magic session last night hadn't let up. After a horrible night's rest, I'd moved to the living room and made a makeshift bed on the couch. It was noisier and brighter, but at least I felt like I was part of the living. There was nothing worse than being holed up in a dark room with no human interaction for days on end.

"No, no. Don't get up." Bertha slung a kitchen towel over her shoulder and walked to the front door.

"Oh, hello, Ted." She stepped back and allowed my boyfriend inside.

Boyfriend. That was an odd word, even if I hadn't said it out loud. It didn't exactly roll off the tongue after this many years, but boy was I excited about it. I'd been married for so long that I'd never imagined I'd have someone new in my life with that title.

"Hey, there, beautiful," Ted whispered and sat on the floor next to the couch.

I didn't have the energy to sit up and could only imagine how unruly I must've looked.

Ted pulled a bouquet from behind his back. They were purple tulips, perfectly shaped and without any blemishes. "I thought these might cheer you up."

I couldn't help but smile. "You remembered my favorite."

"Of course I did," he said, placing the flowers on the edge of the couch. He leaned back and reached for a small bag, pulling out a few cream-filled pastries.

Bertha eyed them hungrily from the kitchen before declaring, "Um, I need to go check on something."

"Hey, why don't you take some of these with you?" Ted offered.

Bertha smiled. "Thanks! These will go good with my nip. I mean, with what I need to go check on." She chuckled a little guiltily, then grabbed a few pastries and disappeared back into the kitchen.

We were alone in the living room to enjoy our small moment together.

Ted swept a stray strand of hair off my cheek. "How are you feeling today?"

I sighed. "The same. This headache is miserable." I was getting tired of saying that.

"What have you tried to knock the edge off?" Ted took a bite of a pastry and held it out to me, offering a bite.

"Oh, no, thank you. I don't feel like eating when my head hurts this badly." I closed my eyes and tried to remember the last time I'd taken ibuprofen. "I haven't taken anything today because it's useless. The headache never goes away. At best it just lightens up a little."

"I brought something for you to try." Ted reached into his pocket and pulled out a small, glass bottle. "It's CBD oil. Have you ever taken any?"

Oh, great. My boyfriend wanted to get me high. "Umm, no. I don't think having a trippy morning is going to get rid of the headache."

Ted laughed and took the last bite of his pastry. "Oh, Mae. This isn't marijuana. It's a chemical found in weed, but it doesn't have THC in it. That's what alters your mental state. It's completely harmless."

I eyed the bottle and then snatched it from Ted's hand. It looked benign enough.

"Well, what the hey." I propped myself up on my elbow and squirted a dropperful into my mouth. "If it's from the earth, it can't be that bad. I prefer herbs, anyway."

"Yes." Ted smiled. "I knew that about you."

The effects of the oil were almost immediate. My headache faded and my body felt lighter as if a weight had been lifted off me. I couldn't believe that something natural could give me this much relief when ibuprofen had hardly put a dent in my pain.

"Wow." I looked at Ted in amazement. "That was amazing. You're amazing."

Ted smiled and kissed me gently on the cheek. "I didn't know it could work that quickly. Do you think your magic responded to it, speeding it up?"

"Maybe so." I sat up and tried to tame my long, wild hair. "I'm not going to overthink it. My head's not pounding and that's all that matters to me."

Ted joined me on the couch and put his arm around me. I leaned against his broad shoulder just as Bertha walked through the living room door.

"Oh, good grief." She rolled her eyes and smirked. "Why don't y'all get a room."

Ted chuckled and waved to Bertha as she grabbed her keys and walked out the front door. "I'll be back this evening. Call if you need me."

Calling Bertha was definitely a last resort. Ever since she'd decided to get a cell phone, Lela and I'd spent hours trying to help her understand the electronic device. When they say you can't teach an old dog new tricks, they were right. Poor Bertha typically held the phone upside down or tried to talk to someone without actually making a call.

"I've got a class later this morning, but before I go, I wanted to ask you a question." Ted turned to face me. "You can say no if you want. But my gut tells me that now's the time to ask. Since you're feeling better, I wondered if you'd go on a date with me. Tonight?"

Whew. I thought he was going to ask me to marry him. What a buildup to such an innocent question.

"Of course, I'd love to." I patted Ted's leg. "Where would you like to go?"

"Let's get dinner." Ted suddenly became very serious. "There's a hidden agenda to our date, though."

"Oh, yeah?" I raised one eyebrow. "What's that?"

"Will you bring Lela if I bring Joseph?" Ted grinned mischievously.

My heart melted. Ted was a man of many surprises, but this one took the cake. His going out of his way to set Lela up with his brother meant the world to me. My sister deserved the very best.

"Yes! I'd love that." I hugged Ted's neck. "Let's make it happen!"

"Alright. It's a date." Ted pulled me close and tenderly kissed my lips. The whole house could have caught on fire and I wouldn't have noticed.

I didn't want him to go, but his history students at the college depended on him. We walked hand-in-hand to the door.

"So we will meet you all at seven at the Mexican restaurant?" Ted kissed my hand.

"Yep. We'll see you there." I waved and stood at the door, watching him walk to his car. As soon as he drove out of sight, I ran to Lela's bedroom and burst in without knocking.

"Uhhh." Lela moaned and shifted underneath her covers. "What do you want?"

"Sorry to interrupt your slumber, but I have some news that'll make you feel better." I plopped down on the edge of the bed and threw the blanket off of Lela's head.

"Ted brought me some CBD oil and it helped take the edge off of my head pain." I shoved the bottle in Lela's face. "Do you want to try some?"

"Ugh. No." She pushed my hand away. "There's no way I could keep that down. Yuck."

"How does a double date sound?" I asked.

"A double date?" Lela opened one eye and squinted in my direction. "With who? Whom? Whatever. I never know which."

"Well, let's see. It would be Ted and me. And you." I counted on my fingers. "Oh, and Joseph."

Lela sat up so quickly that she nearly knocked me off the bed. "Are you serious?"

"As a heart attack." I giggled at her reaction.

Lela jumped out of bed and belched loudly, then moaned and clutched her stomach.

"Whoa." I jokingly waved my hand in front of my face.

"Sorry." Lela laughed. "My stomach's still off."

"You don't say." I stood and turned toward the door.

"Wait, don't go." Lela grabbed my arm. "What will I wear? And what should I talk to him about? Maybe we could make a list of conversation starters."

The panic in my sister's eyes was hilarious and endearing. I hadn't seen her this worked up over a person of the opposite sex since we were in high school, and she had the biggest crush on the captain of the basketball team.

"Lela. Chill." I patted her hand. "You and Joseph hit it off before. Your conversation flowed easily. It'll be the same tonight. Just be yourself."

Lela sighed. "You're right. If he's going to like me, I want it to be genuine and not some misconception of who I truly am."

"That's the spirit." I turned to walk away and then remembered some unfinished business we hadn't had time to discuss. "Let's take a look at those coins Florie warned us about."

"Oh, yeah." Lela followed me into the living room where we removed the board on the wall and peered inside with my phone's flashlight.

"Hmm." I stuck my head in deeper and looked around. "I don't see them."

"I don't either." Lela brushed the dust off her nose. "We did put them in here, right?"

"Yeah, you weren't dreaming that. It made perfect sense for us to put them here with the other items we found on the property." I took one more look for good measure, but the coins weren't in the secret hole, though everything else was just where we'd left them.

"What in the tartar sauce are we going to do?" Lela plopped down on the couch and held her head with both hands.

"Let's try to be rational." I paced the floor. "They could still be here. Maybe Bertha moved them. We'll search the house." There was no point in calling Bertha. She couldn't answer.

We spent the next hour turning the house upside down, looking under furniture, in drawers, and even in the flowerpots on the front porch. The coins were nowhere to be found.

I picked up my phone and reluctantly dialed Bertha's number. After several rings, she finally answered, only to immediately drop the phone onto the floor. The loud crash hurt my ear, and my headache started up again.

"Bertha?" I asked, wondering if she was holding the phone correctly to her ear. Probably not.

"Yes, Mae. I can hear you." Bertha shouted at the top of her lungs. Again, not helping with the headache. I held the phone a foot away from my head.

"Bertha, we've gone over this before." I sighed. "You don't have to shout into the phone for me to hear you."

I put her on speakerphone so Lela could enjoy the ridiculousness of the phone call.

"Okay, Mae." Bertha lowered her voice to the point that I could hardly hear her. "I hear you."

I turned the volume up on my phone. "Listen, I just need to know if you touched those old, Scottish coins. Did you move them from our hiding spot in the living room?"

"Coins? Nope." Bertha must've been holding the phone with her shoulder because now her voice was muffled.

"Are you sure?" I hated to prolong the conversation, but I wanted her to think long and hard. Sometimes she could be a little on the forgetful side.

"I think I'd know if I moved golden coins around in your house." Bertha grunted. "Is that all? I'm in the middle of brewing, ah, something."

Oh, I bet she was.

"That's all we needed, Bertha." I picked the phone up off the table. "Except we won't be home this evening so you better plan on eating dinner at your house."

"No problem. I'm feeling pretty tired, anyway." Bertha hung up the phone without saying bye, which was par for the course with her.

Lil' Stinky and Sally watched us from the kitchen counter. "Do either of you know anything about the coins?"

The skunk lowered his head and Sally curled up into a ball. "That was a big, fat *no*." Lela tapped her fingernails on the table. "Who else would've moved them? Maybe Harriet?"

"I doubt it, but I'll text her." I quickly tapped out a message. "I don't want to interrupt her if she's in the middle of class.

Within thirty seconds, I already had a response.

I haven't touched the coins. Sorry, Mom.

"Let's call Leon. We moved the coins to the hiding place after the renovation, but... I don't know. I'm out of ideas and people to ask. He's the only one who has been near them other than our immediate family," I suggested.

Lela stood and backed away from the table. "That's as good of an idea as any. Maybe he'll have a suggestion for us. Just make sure you don't mention the coins right out in case he has no clue what you're talking about. No need in drawing attention to golden coins worth a butt load of money."

"I'll put him on speakerphone." I quickly pulled up Leon's contact information.

He answered after the first ring.

"Hi, there, Mae." Leon's voice was just as chipper as ever. "How are you today?"

"Hi, Leon." I pushed the phone to the center of the table. "I hope I didn't catch you in the middle of a project."

"Nah, I'm at the hardware store picking up some supplies. Seems like I live here most days." Leon cleared his throat. "What can I do for you?"

"Lela and I are missing some family heirlooms and we wondered if you or some of your workers might have found them." I paused, waiting for Leon's response.

"Oh, I don't know of anything." He paused. "I mean, we found the typical things you might find on an old homestead. Some nails, old bottle tops, things of that nature."

Lela pulled the phone closer to her face. "We're specifically looking for gold coins that have been passed down for many generations." She'd grown impatient with the lack of information.

"The only coins we found were nickels, dimes, and pennies. But I'll certainly ask my men if they saw anything like what you're describing. I had a very small crew working with me because only those who know about magic were allowed on the property."

That was a good point. Leon couldn't afford for normal humans to see the trees producing wood on demand for the project.

"Thank you, Leon." I snatched my phone away from Lela. "Please let us know if they have any additional information."

"No problem, Mae. Have a nice day."

As soon as I hung up, Lela lost her mind.

"Do I have your permission to freak out *now*?" She walked to the front door and out onto the porch.

I jumped up and followed her. "Where are you going?"

"To search the yard." Lela stomped over to the area we'd originally found the coins. "Maybe they're back in the original hiding place."

"It's not like they could've grown legs and walked away." I rolled my eyes at my sister, who sometimes became a little melodramatic.

"Let's think about it for a second." I put my hands on my hips. "Maybe one of us sleepwalked."

"Yeah, or maybe the curse on the coins caused them to move to another location," Lela added.

Each suggestion was more ludicrous than the last, but we were desperate. Neither of us was in the market to be cursed for all of eternity.

"Maybe the animals know something about them," I suggested. It was a desperate hope, but I was grasping at straws at this point.

Within seconds, Lela had summoned multiple species into the backyard. She held her hand out toward them and communicated with them through her mind.

"Nope, they don't know what I'm talking about." Lela shrugged her shoulders.

"Let's look on the bright side," I pointed out. "The curse won't take effect until we die."

Lela spun on her heel and went back toward the house. "Super."

Meh. I tried.

13
LELA

"LET'S TRY THE GHOST." I LOOKED AT MY SISTER AND raised my eyebrows. "Why not? We don't have anything else to go on, and it's worth a shot." Harriet was in class and Bertha said she had some brewing to do.

We all knew what that meant. But it also meant we were alone, which was good for the ghost. Mae had told me she'd had to feed Florie power in order for the specter to appear in front of me, and that it would be too much to try to get her to appear in front of others.

Mae nodded her agreement and we got up. She grabbed the cauldron from its spot beside the fire and put it on the coffee table. "With all the power we have, it seems like you could give her enough to appear in front of Harriet or Bertha." I cocked my head at my sister.

She looked kind of blank. "Yeah, but it feels like I'm giving her a huge amount of power to help. It's kind of exhausting."

"Maybe you should do it more often to help with your headaches." As it was, I was going to have to call sick animals to heal. Or maybe take a trip to the local hospital. I had to be careful about healing humans. For one, I didn't like playing God. But if someone figured out the patients were being magically healed, questions would rise that I couldn't answer. Nobody could. The last thing any of us wanted was scientists nosing around.

A few seconds later, the red-headed ghost appeared. My heart fluttered in fear, but I stamped it back. I'd lost it a little bit the last time I'd seen her, and it'd been crazy embarrassing. I was a mature, responsible granny witch. The last thing I should do is freak out over an innocent ghost.

The ghost walked right up to me as if she had been waiting for this moment. My fear threatened to rear its head but I gritted my teeth and smiled instead. "It's good to see you." My voice sounded steady and strong, thank goodness.

The ghost smiled, her eyes twinkling. "It's nice to see you again, my many times great-granddaughter," she said before turning to Mae and smiling. "It is wonderful to be summoned here. It does get lonely, being a ghost."

"Is there anything else you can tell us about the coins?" I asked. "Or about the original twins?"

Florie sighed and floated toward the fireplace. "Agnes and Margaret. They were practically worshiped by the kin back in Scotland."

"We have family in Scotland?" Mae asked excitedly.

"Well, I haven't been able to keep up with them, but aye, I left many cousins and relatives behind. Their descendants may still be there today."

A thrill ran through me. Scottish cousins. How cool.

"Do you know if any of them have powers?" Mae asked, her eyes wide with excitement.

Florie shrugged. "I'm no sure, but I suspect some do. The original twins had great powers, so it makes sense that some of their descendants would." She looked away, and with her being semi-transparent, it was difficult to tell, but it looked like something definitely bothered Florie when talking about the people she'd left behind in Scotland.

I stepped closer and smiled at her. "You don't have to talk about it if you don't want to."

The ghost smiled and nodded. "Thank you."

Mae and I exchanged looks before standing up. Our mission had just gotten a whole lot more interesting. "What can you tell us about our magic?"

That seemed to get Florie excited. "Do you know about the twin magic?"

"Well, we have powerful magic, which is related to us being twins." Mae looked at me again. "That's about all we know."

"Twins have always been the most powerful." Florie furrowed her brow. "Are you the seventh twins?"

We stared at her blankly. "We have no idea."

"If you are, you probably sucked up all the power in the area. It's a blessing and a curse."

"Yep." I leaned back on the couch. "We must be the seventh. That explains it. There was this big prophecy about our birth. The local coven tried to kill us so we wouldn't take all their power."

Florie nodded wisely. "Yes, you're the second set of seventh, then, as far as I know. It's very difficult to have that much power, and not entirely worth it."

"Is there anything else special about us, as twin witches?" Mae asked.

Florie nodded. "Oh, yes. I'll bet you've figured out you can speak in each other's minds?"

We both nodded eagerly.

"Do you have the ring?" She tapped her finger.

"Yes, we've only used it a few times." I leaned forward. "I can go get it if you'd like."

"No, no. I made that set myself, for my granddaughters. The other set was... lost to me." She looked sad again.

"Anything else?" Mae prompted. "I'm starting to get a little tired."

Florie tapped her lip. "Only twins have the power of healing and water, but you probably knew that."

"No," I whispered. "But it's sure good to know."

Moving quickly enough that I had to fight a jump, Florie snapped her fingers. "Have you found my broom?"

"A broom?" Mae looked as confused as I felt. "What broom?"

"I had a broom that was originally Agnes or Margaret's. Not sure which. The mate to that broom I had to leave in Scotland." Here came the sad face again.

"Was there something special about the broom?" I asked. "Or did it just look like an old broom?"

"It was beautifully carved. It's imbibed with magic. It will last forever without looking worn at all." Florie sighed and turned away, which was weird with her being kind of transparent. I could see her face still, through her body, and the sight was unsettling.

"What could've happened to it?" Mae asked.

"It was with me in the woods when I died. As far as I know, it's still there." She turned back around. "You could summon it. It belongs to you girls now."

"How would we summon it?" Mae asked.

"Well, I simply thought about the broom and held out my hand. Then it would fly to me, as long as it wasn't somewhere like locked in a room or something." She nodded toward the door. "Go out and try to call it to you."

We stepped toward the door, but then I turned back. "Are you coming?"

She looked more transparent than before and smiled, very sadly this time. "I can't. Tied to the cauldron."

Mae stuck her head back through the doorway. "I'll summon you back as soon as we have it. Promise."

It took something out of me to watch Florie disappear. Now I had a sad look on my face.

"Come on." Mae held the door for me. "Let's find this broom."

It was ridiculously easy. We stood on the porch and thought hard about the broom. I tried to summon it the way I summoned the animals. Mae gasped a few seconds later and I opened my eyes.

It was right in front of us, but the thing was *nothing* like I might've expected. The broom hovered in the air in front of us, vibrating slightly. *Move to the left.* I spoke to Mae in her head so the broom wouldn't know what we were doing. As she shifted to the left, I did the same but went to the right. The broom hesitated for half a second, then moved to be in the middle of us again. "It can't choose between us."

"Why is the end carved to look like a parrot?" Mae asked, her voice full of shock. "It makes no sense. If it belonged to someone living in Scotland that many years ago... Did they even know about parrots?"

Reaching out I grabbed the broom, which gave no resistance. It felt warm in my hand, and a hum radiated from it. "Let's go in and ask Florie."

We hurried in, and a few seconds later, Mae had the Scottish woman somewhat visible. "Why a parrot?" I asked first thing. It wasn't what we truly needed to know about the broom, but it was definitely the thing sticking out in my mind.

"Oh, one of the twins was obsessed with parrots," Florie said. "A visitor to the highlands had one. He said he got him off a pirate, but when he left, the parrot stayed." She moved toward the broom and lifted her hand as if to stroke the parrot's head, but then her fingers passed right through.

"I'm sorry, Florie." Mae gave her a sympathetic look.

"What did the other broom look like?" I asked.

"It had a stag's head carved into it like this." She moved back and crossed her arms as if steeling her resolve against wanting to touch the broom.

"What does this thing do?" I asked, sort of changing the subject.

"Well, it cleans of course. Put a little power in it and it'll clean your whole house." She grinned. "But not just the sweeping. This broom will mop, dust, it'll even wash the pots."

I whistled through my teeth. "Where have you been all my life?"

"No joke." Mae took it from me and studied it closely. "This is awesome."

"That's not all." Florie winked at Mae when she turned to look at her. "If you've lost anything, the broom can find it."

Mae and I gaped at each other. "That's convenient timing, discovering the broom just as we desperately needed to find something."

"What have you lost?" she asked.

Mae and I exchanged a glance. "Oh, just a bracelet of Mae's," I said. No way I was telling this poor ghost that we'd lost the very thing that kept her tied to the earth. Or maybe that was the cauldron. Heck, I had no idea. Where did she go when not appearing in front of us? I wasn't sure I wanted to know.

"Just ask it to find lost things. I never was able to get it to do anything more specific than that." She sucked in a breath. "I almost forgot. Never ask it to find lost things when it's not in a confined space. If it goes outside and you ask it to find lost things, it'll disappear. And it doesn't like to return when summoned if it's working like that. Also, don't ask it to clean out there." She shuddered. "It makes it very frantic."

"Why did you have it out in the woods?" I asked.

She looked at me like I was crazy. "I was riding it, of course."

Oh. Of course. She was riding it. What else?

"Please find lost things," I whispered and funneled a tiny bit of power into the broom.

It took off like a shot, and Mae and I both jumped back. It flew right out the window, nearly taking the curtains with it. We watched it go, dismayed.

"Aye, probably should've closed that," Florie said.

A half-hour later, with our combined efforts, we managed to get the broom to come back. This time, we closed all the windows and locked the doors for good measure.

The broom flew around the house, using its handle or bristles to dig into the couch, knock on a floorboard, and dig into a closet. We found an earring I hadn't even realized I was missing, a load of lost coins, some kind of old, but none the ones we needed to find, and a tiny piece of paper with a secret message written on it in what looked to be very childlike writing. The coins were still missing, but at least the broom seemed to be well-behaved.

"Well, that was quite the adventure," Mae said with a sigh, then called Florie back.

I nodded in agreement and looked at Florie. "Mae looks exhausted. I think she needs a nap before our date tonight."

"Sorry, Florie," Mae whispered.

Florie waved sadly as she disappeared. Just as Mae was about to head to her room, Bertha walked in. We regaled her with tales of the broom and she was beside herself excited. The broom was as much her heritage as ours. Harriet's too. Bertha played with the broom, using it to clean while Mae went to nap. When she walked into the kitchen, she called for me. "What is this?"

I looked to see what Bertha was talking about. She held up the little piece of paper.

"A note. It looks like a child wrote it."

She smiled sadly and looked down at the writing. "She did. Susan wrote this when we were little girls. All the other notes we wrote to each other have been lost, probably thrown away."

Bertha sat at the kitchen table and a single tear rolled down her cheek. I sat down next to her and put my arm around her shoulders.

"We'll keep it, Bertha. What does it say?"

"It was a secret language only we knew." She sniffled. "A twin thing."

"Oh, don't I know it. Mae and I kept saying we were going to make one up but we never did."

She read the note as if it was written in perfect English. "Thomas Myers pulled my hair at recess. I think he likes me." With a deep chuckle, she pressed the note to her chest. "I guess he did like her."

Thomas Myers was our grandfather. He'd died in Vietnam.

We sat for a few minutes in silence. "That broom is going to be a good addition to our households," Bertha said. "I don't suppose it found the coins?"

I snorted and got up. "No. I have to go get ready for my date."

Walking to my room to the sound of catcalls from Bertha probably should've annoyed me, but it didn't. I couldn't help but grin.

It was time to get ready for my date with Joseph.

Eek!

. . .

"DON'T BE NERVOUS," Mae whispered as we walked to the door of the restaurant an hour later. We were meeting them here, at the nicest restaurant in town. Well, just outside of town. Blueberry Mountain Tavern. "Bertha said that celebrities come here to eat and stay at the lodge all the time." Mae nodded toward the big luxury hotel on top of the hill. "Supposedly the Kardashians were here last week."

I arched one eyebrow at her. I didn't care one way or another about celebrities, but she had succeeded in distracting me for a moment. "I thought we left L.A.," I said wryly.

She snorted. "You never know. Maybe we'll eat next to Dolly."

Now that was someone I wouldn't mind meeting.

Thirty seconds later, all thoughts of famous people left me. Joseph and Ted stood as the hostess led us to their table. Ted leaned over and pressed a kiss to Mae's cheek as Joseph pulled out the chair across from his. "It's good to see you," he said quietly. "You look lovely, Lela."

I smiled and thanked him before sliding into my seat.

Ted sat down across from Mae, their eyes locked in an intimate conversation that nobody else was privy to.

Joseph cleared his throat and opened the wine menu, breaking the spell between them.

"How has your day been?" He handed the menu to Ted. "You're better at this than I am."

The server approached, and Ted pointed to the menu. He said words, but Joseph had leaned toward me at that exact moment and I lost all sense of his brother. "I can't thank you enough for helping Eleanor."

Waving him off, I took the menu the server handed me. "It was my pleasure. I'd do it a hundred times over. Where is Eleanor tonight? I know she typically stays with Ted when you're busy."

"She's at a friend's house having a dinner play date."

A minute later, a glass of red wine appeared in front of me. Not magic. Just excellent service. *I don't know what to order.*

Mae smiled at her menu. *I'm sure it's all good.*

I really want a cheeseburger but don't want to look like a country mouse.

My sister cleared her throat delicately. *Go with a salad. That's always safe.*

When it was our turn to order, I had a nice salad in mind, all ready to order it, but what came out of my mouth was, "Cheeseburger with fries and the steamed broccoli, please."

Joseph smiled broadly. "I've had their burgers. they're phenomenal." He looked up at the server and grinned. "I'll have the same."

I couldn't take my attention off of him to hear what Mae and Ted ordered, but they were perfectly capable of feeding themselves without any help from me.

Once the server was gone, Ted leaned in and said, "How's the research going for the power share? I tell ya, if there's a way to share without the bad side effects, I'd be very interested in doing it again. After going our whole lives hearing our mom and females on her side of the family, it was *so cool* to have my own magic." His face was so animated. Without saying another word his face told us clearly how much he'd loved it.

"Yeah, if you figure it out, please let me know. I'd love to have powers before Eleanor comes of age to get any. Eleanor's mother was human, and our mother was a witch, so we're not sure if she'll have them or not. I'd like to be prepared."

"And we don't have any female relatives anymore to help her," Ted said. "It's all on us."

"We'd help," I said softly. "I'd help. I'd love to. I'm still learning myself, but hey, Eleanor and I, and *we*," I nodded toward my sister, "could learn together."

Mae nodded eagerly. "I agree. We'd love to."

The server arrived with bread and more wine, interrupting our conversation. We stopped talking about things that might be better left for private. Ted grinned broadly a few minutes later, once we had our entrees. "A little birdie told me that Saturday is your birthday. Joseph and I were hoping you two, along with Harriet and Bertha, would come out to dinner with us."

I gaped at him. "Oh, my gosh, I'd forgotten."

Joseph laughed, a booming, warm, inviting sound that made me want to laugh with him. "You invited me over for dinner on your birthday and forgot about it?"

"No," I protested. "I remembered the date. I forgot the birthday."

He winked. "Now I know your priorities."

Boys, howdy, as Bertha would've said. He really had me pegged.

"Ouch, watch it!" Lela snapped at me after I accidentally stepped on her foot.

Bertha had insisted on driving us to the coven meeting in her truck. When I said I'd drive separately, she'd about had a fit. Lela nor I had the patience to listen to one of Bertha's rants, so we nodded our heads and hopped in the truck when Bertha said it was time to go.

Bertha pulled into the parking lot, and I was surprised to find so many cars already there. "Did we get the time wrong?"

Bertha glanced at her watch. "Uhh, nope. It starts at seven and we're only a few minutes early."

Granny witches, at least the ones in our coven, were notorious for being late. There must've been something about the mountain culture and taking their time.

"You two go on ahead. I'm going to make a call before I come in." Bertha shooed us out.

I closed the truck door and gave Lela a worried look. "She's going to make a phone call? On her own?"

Lela laughed. "Don't ask questions. Bertha's going to do what she wants. Hopefully, she doesn't call and harass some unsuspecting stranger."

When we opened the door to the big cabin for tonight's meeting, it was dark inside. What in the world?

"Maybe they're all out back," Lela suggested. "It's a nice night for an outdoor meeting."

I shrugged and pushed the door all the way open as the lights flipped on and everyone yelled, "Surprise!"

Lela jumped back and grabbed my arm, and I screamed. Holy guacamole. We hadn't been expecting a surprise party.

A huge banner read, 'Happy Birthday Mae & Lela!' Everyone erupted in applause. Until Ted had reminded us the night before last, we'd completely forgotten that our forty-second birthday was this weekend and we *certainly* hadn't expected this.

Bertha stepped out from the back of the room with a huge grin on her face. "I told you I had to make a call." She winked, and we burst into laughter.

I looked around the room at all of the smiling faces as Harriet came forward from the crowd and hugged my neck. "Happy birthday, Mom."

"Hey, sweetie." I gave her a good squeeze. "I thought you were stuck on campus all week with meetings and class."

Harriet laughed. "You don't think I'd miss my own mother's surprise party, do you?"

I turned to see who had just placed their hand on my lower back, though I knew all too well that it was Ted.

"Happy birthday, beautiful." He kissed me on the cheek and handed me a small, pink gift bag. "I still want to take you out on Saturday for a nice dinner, but I thought I'd go ahead and give you your gift since I'm an impatient child."

I laughed. "Aww, you didn't have to buy me anything. The CBD oil was the best gift ever."

Ted chuckled. "Oh, I think you'll like this one too. Go ahead, open it!"

I pulled out the tissue paper and revealed a small pewter box with a tiny dragonfly on top. I gasped as I opened the lid to find a delicate, gold bracelet.

"I know how much you love jewelry, so I wanted to find something you could wear every day." Ted raised his eyebrows, waiting for my response to his gift.

Pulling the bracelet out of the box, I handed it to Ted. "I love it. It's perfect. Will you put it on for me?"

I thrust my wrist forward, and Ted clasped the bracelet around my wrist.

"Beautiful," he said, softly as he looked into my eyes.

The room was suddenly so quiet as if everyone had left us alone in our little bubble.

Then Bertha cleared her throat and everyone started talking again so it broke the spell between us. "How about you girls come over and see your cake?"

Looking around the room, I finally spotted Lela chatting with Joseph. Precious. He'd come to her surprise party.

"Sure, Bertha." I looped my arm through hers. "You lead the way."

Lela and I followed Bertha to the other side of the room where a three-tiered cake displayed in the center of the table. One half had red icing and the other had yellow.

"Get it?" Bertha laughed. "It represents y'all's hair color."

We all laughed and praised the inventive cake.

"Birthday girls, make a wish!" yelled a voice from the crowd.

We both closed our eyes and made a silent wish before blowing out our candles. My wish was simple. I hoped that my relationship with Ted would continue to grow.

When we opened our eyes, everyone clapped and cheered. I felt like such a celebrity.

"Thank you all so much," Lela shouted as she threw her arms up in the air.

I echoed her sentiments, feeling incredibly grateful for my friends and family who had come together to make this day special for us.

"Congratulations on another year around the sun." Yvonne, the granny witch nurse we'd discovered at the nursing home, patted my back.

"Thank you, Yvonne." I swallowed a bite of cake. "How's everything going at the nursing home? Have you been using your healing powers?" We'd recently learned that Yvonne had a twin sister who had died at birth. It was the only explanation for her healing powers since Florie had said only twins had it.

Yvonne sighed. "My supervisors were highly suspicious after a whole floor of patients were healed on the same day. So I'm trying to lay low. I do, however, offer the occasional healing when I'm alone with a patient who's suffering. I can't stand to see them hurting."

I admired Yvonne for her compassionate care of the elderly. What an admirable job. "You're doing a fantastic job. The residents are lucky to have you around."

Someone's hand waving over Yvonne's shoulder pulled my attention away. It was Leon. I tossed my hand in the air and warily waved back. I hoped he wasn't about to give me some of the same creepy weirdo vibes he'd given Lela.

"Hey, there, Mae." Leon made his way to my side, and I smiled at Yvonne as she moved on to chat with someone else.

"Leon." I forced a smile. "Thank you for coming to the party."

"Oh, I wouldn't miss it for the world" He eyed Lela as he spoke, and it gave me the heebie-jeebies. "Did you ever find those coins you lost?"

"No, we didn't." I shoved my hands into my pockets and looked around for Ted. Surely, he'd come to rescue me from this uncomfortable conversation.

"Well, maybe you could ask the coven since everyone's here," Leon suggested. "You never know, maybe someone will have a helpful idea.

What a nice suggestion. Maybe Leon was a good guy, albeit a little on the awkward side. "Thank you. I'll do that." How had we not noticed his weirdness before? It was like he'd changed.

I joined Lela and Joseph, who'd found a corner to sit and chat.

"Hey, sorry to interrupt." I grinned, hoping Lela wouldn't use her animal powers to have a bear maul me for my intrusion. "Lela, can I chat with you for a moment?"

Lela smiled at Joseph and excused herself. "What is it?" she hissed. "Can't you see that Joseph and I are getting to know each other better? Why didn't you just talk to me telepathically?"

"Yes, I see that you were in the middle of a conversation. That's exactly why I knew you wouldn't focus on my words if Joseph was in front of you." I raised an eyebrow and Lela nodded, knowing that I was right. "I just wanted to know if you think we should ask the coven about the missing coins?" I asked.

"Why would we do that?" Lela looked confused.

"Well, maybe they'd have a suggestion for us." I shrugged my shoulders. "Who knows? Someone might have seen them somewhere."

"I guess it wouldn't hurt." Lela turned and walked back to Joseph.

I scanned the room for Constance and found her near the cake table with George. I explained that I needed to make an announcement. She didn't have any questions for me this time, which was a relief. George whistled loudly and the noise level quickly died down.

"Hey, everyone." I stood on a chair so the coven could see who was talking. "First, thank you all so much for throwing this party for us. We couldn't have been more surprised, and we're so thankful for your friendship and support."

The crowd cheered as I blushed.

"Since we're all together, I do have one piece of coven business to discuss." I rubbed my sweaty hands together. Public speaking had never been my favorite subject in school. Too nerve-wracking. "Lela and I have lost some coins that have been passed down through our family for many generations. They're very old and unique, with an emblem of

Mary Queen of Scots on the front. We've had no luck in finding them on or around our property, and everyone we've asked hasn't seen them. We are hopeful that one of you might know something or have a suggestion for us. If you do, please come find one of us. Thank you."

I hopped down from the chair and everyone returned to their previous conversations, probably now punctuated with curiosity about the old coins and what might've happened to them.

Within a few minutes, Cindy, the granny witch who was also a cop, pulled me aside. "Hey, about those coins. Can't you do some kind of locator spell?"

A locator spell. Duh. Why hadn't we thought of that?

"You know, Cindy, that's an excellent idea." I smoothed my long braid down my back. "Surely we could use the scrying spell we used a while back when we were trying to figure out who was after us."

Cindy smiled and slapped me on the back, a little harder than I would've liked. Man, that woman was strong. "Glad I could be of service to you. Happy birthday, by the way."

"Thanks, Cindy."

Not wanting to be rude, I waited another hour before I convinced Lela to come home with me and try a locator spell on the coins. She asked Joseph if he'd drive her home, and to my dismay, she'd invited him in. I wasn't sure how I felt performing magic in front of someone I barely knew, but I reminded myself that he was Ted's brother and seemed to be a standup guy. Besides, I was in a coven now. It was time to get used to doing magic in front of others.

I glanced at my phone and was surprised to see that it was already eleven. No wonder I was so worn out. "Alright, if we're going to do this, we need complete silence from onlookers.

Bertha, Joseph, and Harriet nodded in agreement and found a seat in the living room. I hoped Ted wouldn't feel left out, but I hadn't planned on having an audience.

I turned to Lela. "Do we have anything that the coins touched? I know the box they were in is gone, but without the coins or something that recently touched them, I'm not sure how well this locator spell will work."

Lela shook her head. "I don't know of anything. I mean, our hands touched them. But that was weeks ago."

Sighing, I flipped through the grimoire until I found the spell used to locate lost items or people. As I suspected, we needed a sample of the item or something closely related to it.

"You might need one of my maps," Bertha piped in from the living room.

Ugh. She was right. How else would we find the location of the coins?

"It's a good thing I left one here at the house." She stood and walked to the utility closet and retrieved the rolled-up map of Wears Valley and Townsend.

Spreading the map out flat on the dining room table, Bertha gave us a thumbs up. Somehow, it didn't give me any more encouragement that this was going to work.

"Here." Lela offered. "Use my hand and I'll think about the coins as you perform the spell."

It was as good of an idea as any, so I agreed. Lela placed her hand, palm up, in the center of the map. I held my hand over the table and repeated the words listed in the grimoire. At first, nothing happened. After a few seconds, though, the table rumbled as if there were an earthquake.

Lela's eyes grew wide and she looked up at me for reassurance. I winked and kept repeating the spell.

A squeal from the living room broke my concentration. I looked up just in time to see a ferret run across the floor and jump onto the table. Lela glanced down at the long, furry rodent and screamed.

This, in turn, scared the ferret and he snatched the map out from underneath Lela's hand, ran over to the couch, and landed in Joseph's lap.

Lela looked up at me in shock. "Joseph's presence is messing with my magic again," she whispered.

What an absolute mess. Not only was the locator spell a total bust at that point, we now had to deal with a psychotic ferret and my sister's inability to control her magic.

Awesome.

15
LELA

My phone pinged from the counter as Mae and I stared at the stupid map on the kitchen table. We'd tried every which way from Sunday and back again to Thursday. Nothing was working to help find the coins.

"We have to face the facts," I said as I grabbed my phone. "Scrying isn't going to do anything. We're on our own."

Mae muttered something under her breath as I checked my texts. This one was from George. I hadn't heard from him in a while.

Lela, question for you. Can you call me? Too much to type.

I showed Mae. "I hope it's not like a date thing."

"You've had three guys interested in you since we moved here." Mae waved her finger at me. "Some-how, you bring this on yourself."

I hit George's icon to call him as I rolled my eyes at my sister. So I'd had a few guys interested in me. So what? Back in LA I had plenty of guys who'd wanted to date me. Although, I had to admit that I'd experienced more drama with men in Tennessee than I ever had in California.

He answered on the first ring. "Lela, hey. Thank you for calling."

"Of course. What's up?" I sat next to Mae and leaned in close so she could hear.

"Hey, so, my brother-in-law owns Townsend Coin and Pawn. Some guy came in with one of the coins. He wanted to know if Spencer would buy it or not."

I put the phone on speaker. "George, you're on speaker with me and Mae. Two questions. One, how do you know it was one of our coins, and two, do you know who it was?"

"Well, I'd stopped by to ask if he'd seen anything like it. He managed to pinpoint the specifics of the day and find it on the camera." George sucked in a deep breath.

"What is it, George?" Mae asked. "What don't you want to say?"

"It was Leon. He tried to sell the coin. And my brother-in-law, he knows coins. He knew what it was the minute Leon showed it to him. He couldn't buy it because it's worth so much that Spencer had to say no."

My heart sank into my stomach. Leon was the thief. He'd been acting weird but this was devastating. This was a betrayal in the deepest sense. "We should've known," I whispered. "He was the only person outside of the family who knew about them."

Mae and I were both quiet for a second, trying to absorb the information George had provided.

"Lela," Mae said finally. "Do you think we should confront him?"

I took a deep breath, thinking about what it would mean if we did that. Finally, I nodded my head in agreement. We had to know the truth. Why would he do this? Was it just for the money?

I didn't want to date Leon. Heck, I didn't even want to be his friend, not really. But I had to find out. "Let's go talk to him," I said. "George, thank you so much. You're a good friend."

"Ladies, I don't think you should confront him alone. Call Ted, but I'd be happy to go along. Just to make sure Leon doesn't do anything crazy."

Mae nodded once. "Sounds reasonable," she whispered.

"We'll text you the when and where, okay?"

He agreed, so I hung up the phone.

Mae and I stared at the table for a second, totally blown away. "Leon," she whispered.

"Leon what?" Bertha asked as she came into the room. She'd been in the bathroom a suspiciously long time. She sat across from us at the table, and I leaned in to try to smell her breath.

I couldn't tell from here.

"Leon is the one who stole the coins," Mae said. "George's brother-in-law has footage of Leon bringing one in to try to sell it."

Bertha leaned back in her seat and put her hand over her gaping mouth. "Leon."

It took us a good fifteen minutes to get over our shock and formulate a plan. While Mae called Ted to ask for his and maybe Joseph's help, I called George to fill him in.

George liked the plan. "I think Spencer will go for it. Let me call him."

Bertha had known just the potion. "Here it is, and it's a quick brew." It was easy enough. We threw the ingredients together and said the words in the grimoire, and soon enough we had ourselves a bonafide truth potion.

An hour later, Eleanor was with Bertha and Harriet cooking dinner while Joseph and I sat in the back of Ted's truck, sitting really close together.

Not a bad thing. Not at all.

My phone pinged, and I read the text. "George says Spencer called Leon and Leon is on his way there now. We're good to go."

"We're almost there," Ted said. "I'll drop you off and then park around the building."

Mae squeezed Ted's hand on the gear shifter between them. "I'll let you in the back."

We scurried out of the car at Townsend Coin and Pawn and straight inside. "Hello," a tall man said. "I'm Spencer." He looked over our shoulders, out the window. "Quick, into the back. He just pulled in."

George was back there and had already let Ted in. He nodded at us and gestured to a corner. We pressed ourselves against the wall and waited.

My heart thumped a salsa rhythm in my chest. Partially because of the threat of Leon coming in, but also because I was pressed *all* up against Joseph. As in, from shoulder to knees.

It was like standing against the wall. He was as firm and steady as he could be.

Seconds later, Spencer opened the door and stepped aside. "Come on in, Leon, we'll take a look at those coins. Have you gotten rid of any of them yet?"

"No, I haven—" He stopped short in the doorway and gaped at us. "Lela." His eyes darted to my sister. "Mae. What are you doing here?"

I darted forward and snatched the plastic bag out of his hand. "We'd like to ask you the same thing."

George, Ted, and Joseph moved forward, corralling Leon away from the door. "Have a seat," Joseph said in an impossibly deep and threatening voice.

Be still my heart.

"Drink this." Mae set the small vial on the table in front of Leon. "Don't try any funny business like trying to pour it out. We've got several vials."

"And we'll make you take it if we have to."

Leon sighed. "This is a truth potion?"

I nodded.

Mae said, "Yep."

"This isn't necessary. I'll tell you what happened and why I did what I did."

"Take it anyway." I tried not to bare my teeth at him.

Leon uncorked the vial and downed the liquid with a grunt. "Oh, it's minty."

"Bertha said it takes about thirty seconds to work." I looked at my watch and let it tick down about forty-five seconds for good measure. "Okay. Now you can tell us what in the world possessed you to steal our coins."

I opened the bag and looked inside. "Is this all of them?"

"Yes, I was very careful with them." He scratched his throat and swallowed. "My throat burns."

A knock on the door interrupted us, but it was Officer Cindy. "Thanks for coming," I said.

She sat across from Leon and arched an eyebrow at him.

"Tell us why." Ted squeezed Leon's shoulder. "Spill it."

"When I got powers, what you saw was that I could levitate. What you didn't see was what happened later." He pursed his lips. Was he going to stop talking?

I pulled another vial out of my bag to maybe dose him again, but it was ruined. "Bertha was right." Holding it up, I showed the others that the potion had turned black. "She told us the truth potion has a very short shelf life."

"What happened later?" I asked after putting the potion back. We'd have to rely on him telling the truth. Maybe some of the potion was still working.

"I discovered I could touch things and glimpse little visions about its past. Who the object had belonged to, where it had been, and so on."

"So how does that relate to the coins?" I asked. "Make it make sense."

"I was at your house when I discovered this new power. I knew about your hiding place, of course, I'd helped you install it." He rubbed his eyes. "I touched your cauldron, and it showed me the coins going into the hiding place I'd helped you build. So, I couldn't stop myself from looking. I opened the hiding place, and the first time I touched the coins, I saw so much history. I've mostly been keeping them at home, safe. I couldn't stop myself from touching each one. Eventually, the visions stopped and I looked up the coins online. I was shocked to discover their value." A tear rolled down his cheek. "I wanted to give them back but the lure of that much money was more than I could resist. I just couldn't do it."

"So, you came here and tried to sell ancient, incredibly valuable coins." George rolled his eyes. "Smart. You could've at least gone to Knoxville."

Leon shrugged one shoulder then he deflated a little. "I wish I could go back."

"You can't. And I have your confession. Are you going to cooperate at the station or what?"

Before he could reply, I put my finger in his face. "Let me add, you'll never get powers again, not from us. And while we can't technically speak for Constance, I'll go out on a limb and say you're disinvited to any future coven meetings."

Leon hung his head. "I'll cooperate. I've never stolen anything before."

Cindy slapped handcuffs on him and bustled him out of the back office.

"Are you really going to press charges?" George asked.

I glanced at Mae. "Probably not, but he needs a good wake-up call."

Mae nodded. "Let him go through getting arrested. He'll think twice next time."

16

MAE

AFTER THE DRAMA OF THE DAY BEFORE, MY HEADACHE had returned tenfold. Lela had frequented the bathroom all night, so I assumed she wasn't feeling well, either.

Tapping on her bedroom door, I hoped she was awake, "Lela? You okay?"

A grunt alerted me to the fact that she was still alive, so I opened the door quietly. "I guess you're feeling like poop, as well."

Lela sat up in bed as Lil' Stinky wriggled out from underneath the sheets. "My stomach feels like I swallowed a cup full of nails."

Yuck. That didn't sound pleasant.

"I'm sick of being sick." I leaned against the door-frame and crossed my arms. "Why don't we try another linking spell? Surely there's a way to offload some of this magic without being physically connected."

Lela sighed. "If you have the energy to drag my lifeless body to the kitchen, I'm in."

Now that she mentioned it, Lela's face was extremely pale. I walked to her side and allowed her to hold onto my arm as we made our way to the kitchen. Lil' Stinky refused to leave Lela's side and Sally shimmied out of her container as soon as we entered the room.

"Good morning, little friend." I sat Lela down at a dining room table and scooped Sally into my hand. "You can help me prepare the spell."

I placed Sally on the kitchen counter and opened the grimoire. I flipped through the pages for a spell that could help us without permanently linking our magic together. Could we be so lucky as to find one? After a few moments, I found what we were looking for—a temporary power-sharing spell that might work with parts of the original linking spell.

"We'll have to test it first," Lela said, her voice weak and raspy.

I glanced back down at the spell. Why did everything have to be so complicated? I supposed that we should count our blessings and all of the other cliche sayings that addressed feeling sorry for oneself. Instead, I just wanted to feel normal again.

"The best way to ensure we're not linked physically would be to perform the spell with everyone present. That way, we could do a benign test to see if we're linked like before instead of waiting for someone to injure themselves, and we all end up at the emergency room at the same time."

"So a coven meeting, then?" Lela laid her head on the table. "Ugh, I don't know if I can."

If we didn't get her help soon, I'd have a Weekend at Bernie's situation on my hands.

I rubbed my head and sent out a quick text to the members who had volunteered before, minus Leon, of course. They all agreed to meet us in an hour, which gave us enough time to shower and eat a little breakfast. Though Lela insisted she only wanted coffee.

When we arrived at the meeting, everyone was there except Bertha. Ted had decided to bring Joseph along. He rushed to my side, "You don't look so good." He turned to Lela. "Neither do you. Here, come take a seat. I hope you all don't mind that Joseph came with me. He was at my house when your text came through."

He led us both to chairs at the front of the room and squeezed my shoulder. "This is going to work. Think positively."

Bless Ted. He was always optimistic, no matter the circumstances.

"Am I late?" Bertha burst through the door, fashionably late as always. "This stupid phone didn't tell me that you all were meeting. I just happened to look down and see the invitation while I was in the bathroom."

The coven members snickered as Lela and I shared a concerned glance. Poor Bertha had put her phone on silent again. Too bad there was no time for a geriatric lesson on phone use.

"Glad you made it." I grinned at Bertha and then turned to the group. "Lela and I are really sick again, so I searched for a solution in the grimoire. It looks like we can combine two spells and, hopefully, share our magic without linking physically."

"Is everyone okay with trying again?" Lela weakly asked. "We'll do a quick test after the spell to ensure we're not going to share each other's physical wounds and ailments."

Joseph stepped forward. "Do you mind if I join in this time?"

"Not at all," Lela croaked. She looked at me. *Why does he have to see me like this?*

Hopefully, it's not for long. I squeezed her arm.

The crowd nodded their heads in agreement, so I wasted no time in opening the grimoire and repeating the words for the first spell. The power in the room shifted, and I looked around for signs of anyone in distress. They all continued to stand as they had before with no apparent reactions or issues.

Great.

I moved on to the second portion of the combined spell. This time, once the words were spoken, the same purple mist appeared and encircled Lela and me. The cool sensation felt wonderful against my head, but the mist quickly shifted and surrounded the volunteers.

"Whoo-whee!" Bertha exclaimed as she raised her hands in the air as if she were on a roller coaster at an amusement park.

She was enjoying the sensation a little too much.

Once the mist dissipated, my headache completely disappeared. Sweet relief.

Lela stood to her feet, color rushing back to her cheeks. "Ahh, that's so much better." She stretched and turned to me. "Did it work for you, too?

"I feel like a new woman." I hugged Lela's neck and then turned my attention to the volunteers.

Ted's fire-making ability had returned, as evidenced by how he'd stepped to the side and proceeded to create fireballs out of thin air. Men.

Joseph watched in awe as his brother manipulated fire. He looked down at his own hands. "Umm, guys?"

We all turned to look at Joseph just as a gust of wind shot up from the palm of his hands, blowing his hair back. "How do I stop this?" Joseph waved his hands frantically in the air as the wind encircled him, lifting his shirt, which I don't think Lela minded.

"Calm your mind, Joseph, I instructed. "Take a deep breath and tell the wind to stop."

After a few moments, Joseph harnessed the power and the wind disappeared.

"Looks like it worked." I sat the grimoire in the seat and pulled out a pocketknife I'd found in one of the kitchen drawers. "Now we need to test it."

Lela took a step back. "Not it."

I laughed. "I'll take one for the team this time. Is everyone ready?"

They all nodded in agreement, though several had concerned looks on their faces. Harriet squeezed my shoulder and Bertha looked worried. I didn't blame them. The last time we were linked they'd received a deep gash on their hands out of the blue, which had to have been terrifying.

Not wanting to delay the suspense any longer, I opened the blade and poked my index finger. I watched as a perfectly round pearl of blood rose to the surface.

"Okay, check your fingers," I instructed. "Any pain? Bleeding?"

To our relief, no one displayed physical manifestations. We'd done it! We were successfully linked and finally felt like our old selves.

I'D JUST DOZED off that night when a sound in the living room jolted me awake. I sat upright and pulled the covers up to my chin. The shuffling noise moved closer and closer to my bedroom door until, finally, the door swung open.

"Mom? I need your help." Harriet's voice was shrill, but I couldn't see her anywhere.

Reaching over to turn on my bedside lamp, I allowed my eyes to adjust to the light. "I don't see you, Harriet. Where are you?"

Harriet cried. "Something weird's happening, Mom. Please, help me."

I jumped up and paced the room frantically, trying to make sense of it all. I yelled Harriet's name and she responded even louder. "Mom! Mom! I'm so scared."

My worst nightmare was something happening to my baby, and here we were, in the middle of the night, both of us panicking.

Lela burst into the room with Lil' Stinky and Sally right on her heels. "What in tarnation is going on in here?"

"Aunt Lela, please help me!" Harriet wailed.

"Is that Harriet?" Lela looked around the room. "Where is she?"

Tensions continued to rise until the reality of the situation crashed over me. It was her powers. "It's your power. You're invisible."

Lela reached her hands out, trying to find Harriet. But her body was not only invisible to the naked eye, but we also couldn't touch her. "Harriet, your mom's right. Try to calm down."

Harriet had cried so hard she was basically hyperventilating at that point. "I'm trying," she cried.

"Listen to me, sweetheart." I turned toward the direction of Harriet's voice. "This is your power, your gift. I know it's terrifying, but we just need to teach you how to harness and control it. Breathe with me."

I inhaled deeply, held it for a few seconds, then slowly released all of the air from my lungs. Listening closely, I could hear Harriet's breath releasing at the same time.

"That's wonderful, honey." I took a few more breaths in and slowly, but surely, Harriet's body came into view.

Once she had completely formed in front of our eyes, she collapsed onto the bed. Her cheeks were tear-stained and her eyes were bloodshot. "That wasn't fun."

"No, it wasn't." I wrapped her up in my arms and held her tight. "But look at how brave you were. You faced your fear and regained control of your power."

Lela smiled, proud of Harriet's strength.

"I'm never turning invisible again," she said with a laugh.

"I wonder if anyone else has had problems with their powers tonight." I unplugged my phone from its charger and texted the group. Within minutes, there were several responses. One person said that it was like their powers suddenly went into hyperdrive.

"Everyone we shared our power with had the same issue." I tossed my phone onto the bed. "What in the world changed?"

Lela joined us on the bed while Lil' Stinky and Sally watched us from my dresser. She fiddled with her earring, deep in thought. "We gave them our extra magic, so you'd think that we ultimately control it."

I rolled over to face Lela. "Yeah, I guess so. But how could we cause a surge in energy if we were sleeping?"

Gasping, I sat straight up. "It was me. I must've blasted everyone with extra power. Not on purpose, of course."

"Why was it you?" Lela asked. "How do you know?"

"I just remembered my dream from earlier. Someone had been trying to attack us, so I tried to stop them with a burst of water." I grabbed my phone and sent out a text to the group.

I'M SO SORRY, everyone. I had a nightmare and must've inadvertently directed my magic out to all of you.

. . .

WITHIN SECONDS, Bertha responded in all caps.

THAT SOUNDS LIKE A

PREMONITION DREAM. &MY GREAT GRAND-MOTHER HAD THEM AND HER POWERS$ WOULD ALWAYS GO

HAYWIRE WHEN SHE DID.

ONCE I INTERPRETED Bertha's jumbled-up text, I wondered how she had typed a response so quickly. It would remain one of life's great mysteries.

"Bertha says it must've been a premonition dream. I don't know what that means, and I'm too tired to try and figure it out." I rubbed Harriet's cheek with my finger. "Would you like to sleep with me tonight?"

She nodded her head and crawled up to a pillow.

"I guess we'll head back to our beds." Lela scooped Lil' Stinky and Sally up off of the dresser. "Should I read you a bedtime story so you don't have any more nightmares?"

I rolled my eyes. "I'm good, thanks."

Harriet fell asleep within seconds, obviously exhausted from the energy spent disappearing, reappearing, and crying her poor heart out.

Just as I felt my body slipping into slumber, a familiar voice whispered in my ear. The Scottish accent was undeniable. It was Florie.

"Please break my curse."

I SET THE BOTTLE OF WINE BACK IN THE BUCKET OF ICE and handed Joseph his glass. Mae had helped me create just about the most romantic date ever.

Joseph and I were surrounded by the smell of burning wood and the crackling of a fire that Mae had helped me start. The warmth of the flames was comforting on this unusually chilly September evening.

We sat together on a large rug in front of the fireplace, with pillows behind us for extra comfort. I had set up a small table with a cheese plate, some crackers, and a bottle of red wine.

Joseph and I laughed and talked as we enjoyed our picnic in front of the fire. "Did you always want to be a dentist?" I asked as I sipped my wine.

He smiled and nodded. "Yes, ever since I was a little boy. I love the feeling of helping people and making a difference in their lives."

I smiled and took another sip of my wine. It was so nice to just be together and talk about our lives and dreams. Things had been so hectic lately and it felt good to just relax and enjoy the moment.

"What about you? How did you become a doula?" He touched my hand with one finger, sending a bolt of electricity up my arm.

"Well, I started as a nurse. Then I got a job in labor and delivery. I didn't like some of the hospital policies, which I won't bore you with right now, but essentially I decided my nurse training would be better served as a doula." I paused and thought about my practice back in California. "If things ever calm down here, I really want to take on some clients. I miss my work."

He opened his mouth to say something, but a knock on the door interrupted him.

"Weird," I said. "Harriet and Mae are hanging in the camper tonight. Maybe it's one of them."

I hurried over to the door and flung it open. "What's —Oh. You're not my sister."

"No, but I think I may be your uncle."

I couldn't help but stare at the man in complete confusion. We had no uncles. Our only living relative was Bertha. "How would that be possible?"

"I'm your father's half-brother."

Oh. Well, okay. That was new.

Maybe my drama with men wasn't over. At least this time he wouldn't be asking for a date.

ALSO BY L.A. BORUFF

Witching After Forty (Paranormal Women's Fiction)

A Ghoulish Midlife

Cookies For Satan (*A Christmas Novella*)

I'm With Cupid (*A Valentine's Day Novella*)

A Cursed Midlife

Birthday Blunder

A Girlfriend For Mr. Snoozerton

A Haunting Midlife

An Animated Midlife

Faery Odd Mother

A Killer Midlife

A Grave Midlife

A Powerful Midlife

A Wedded Midlife

Fanged After Forty (Paranormal Women's Fiction)

Bitten in the Midlife

Staked in the Midlife

Masquerading in the Midlife

Karma's Sense

Karma's Stake

Karma's Source

<u>Shifting Into Midlife</u> (Paranormal Women's Fiction)

Pack Bunco Night

Alpha Males and Other Shift

The Cat's Meow

<u>Midlife Mage</u> (Paranormal Women's Fiction)

Unfazed

Unbowed

Unsaid

<u>An Immortal Midlife</u>

<u>An Immortal Midlife</u> (Paranormal Women's Fiction)

COMPLETE SERIES

Series Boxed Set

Fatal Forty

Fighting Forty

Finishing Forty

<u>Immortal West</u> (Paranormal Women's Fiction)

Undead

<u>Hybrid</u>

<u>Fae</u>

<u>The Meowing Medium</u>

<u>The Meowing Medium</u> (Paranormal Cozy)

COMPLETE SERIES

Series Boxed Set Coming Soon

<u>Secrets of the Specter</u>

<u>Gifts of the Ghost</u>

<u>Pleas of the Poltergeist</u>

<u>An Unseen Midlife</u> (Paranormal Women's Fiction Reverse Harem)

<u>Bloom In Blood</u>

<u>Dance In Night</u>

<u>Bask In Magic</u>

<u>Surrender In Dreams</u>

ABOUT L.A. BORUFF

L.A. (Lainie) Boruff lives in East Tennessee with her husband, three children, and an ever growing number of cats. She loves reading, watching TV, and procrastinating by browsing Facebook. L.A.'s passions include vampires, food, and listening to heavy metal music. She once won a Harry Potter trivia contest based on the books and lost one based on the movies. She has two bands on her bucket list that she still hasn't seen: AC/DC and Alice Cooper. Feel free to send tickets.

ABOUT LORRAINE COOKE

Sarah Seaton Myers, writing as Lorraine Cooke, resides in East Tennessee near the gorgeous Great Smoky Mountains with her husband and four children. She is often found purchasing a new house plant and dreaming up home remodeling projects (both to her husband's dismay). She is a graduate of Maryville College and holds a B.A. in Business and Organizational Management. After spending some time as an HR Professional, she felt God's calling, leading her to transition into a full-time homeschooling mom. When she is not teaching her children or writing, she enjoys photography, nature study, reading, hiking, and traveling with her family.

ALSO BY LORRAINE COOKE

Wears Valley Witches

Next of Twin

Twinnin' Aint Easy

Since You Twin Gone

AS SARAH SEATON MYERS

The Buried Reserve

Below

**Letters From Papaw: Stories From Cades Cove and the
Great Smoky Mountains**